EAST LIBERTY

EAST LIBERTY

Joseph Bathanti

Banks Channel Books
Simpsonville, South Carolina

For Joan, Jacob and Beckett
and
in memory of
Philip DeLucia

Also by Joseph Bathanti

Communion Partners

Anson County

The Feast of All Saints

This Metal

About the Carolina Novel Award

Established in 1996 to encourage excellence in fiction writing, the Carolina Novel Award is given every other year to a Carolina author for an unpublished novel chosen in open competition.

Joseph Bathanti is the third winner of the Carolina Novel Award. For the first two winners, both first-time novelists, the award launched a prose fiction career with a major national publisher.

The first winner was Susan S. Kelly, of Greensboro, North Carolina, for *How Close We Come*, a literary novel about women's friendships. Banks Channel Books published its edition and then sold the rights to Warner Books, which re-issued it first in hardcover and then in trade paperback. Warner Books also purchased a second novel, *Even Now*, from Kelly. *How Close We Come* is under option for a TV film, and a German-language edition of the novel has been published.

The second recipient of the Carolina Novel Award, Judith Minthorn Stacy, of Mooresville, North Carolina, won for her comic novel, *Styles By Maggie Sweet*. Banks Channel Books published its edition and then sold rights to HarperCollins, which re-issued it in hardcover under the title *Maggie Sweet*. Several foreign rights were also sold. HarperCollins also purchased the sequel to *Maggie Sweet* from Stacy.

Acknowledgments

Portions of this novel appeared, in appreciably different form, in the following: *Asheville Poetry Review*, as well as in the author's poetry collection, *This Metal* (St. Andrews Press, 1996).

EAST LIBERTY

CHAPTER 1

My mother's name is Francesca Renzo, but she goes by Francene, which she insists I call her. On her bedroom wall is a framed black-and-white still photograph from the 1934 movie *Viva Villa*, starring Wallace Beery. Wearing a sombrero and favoring Oliver Hardy more than Pancho Villa, Beery is second from the left, flanked by two gypsy-looking women and another dubious Mexican, bandoliered and also wearing a sombrero. The picture is enshrined on the wall not because Beery was one of the leading men of the day, but because the torchy, lean, smirking brunette in the revealing black dress, Angelina Colaizzi, grew up on Luna Street in the heart of East Liberty.

Angelina is very pretty, but in a hard way like Marlene Dietrich in *The Blue Angel* or even Greta Garbo. She actually looks a little like Francene. Even in the picture, it's obvious she has that unmistakable East Liberty smart mouth and chip on her shoulder, that she's about to lash out at the other characters whose expressions indicate they will not have an adequate comeback. I don't know if Angelina was ever in another movie. But in 1955, she is the featured celebrity on Italian Day at Kennywood, Pittsburgh's ancient amusement park, and Francene and I are there.

Fifty years old and looking nothing like the girl in the picture, Angelina lounges at a picnic table in one of the pavilions, chatting and signing autographs, drinking lime-colored Canadian Club and sours. She wears sunglasses and a babushka and smokes cigarettes through a long plastic filter that looks like a pipe stem. She is pudgy, but still nice looking. In fact the extra weight has stripped her of that *Viva Villa* hardness and given her the more ample looks of somebody like Shelley Winters. We sit at the table with her for a little while. Francene is intent on having a discussion with her about the movies. But everyone is after her, and finally Francene settles for an autograph.

The pavilion is situated under the biggest dip in the Jackrabbit, Kennywood's notorious rollercoaster. Every so often the cars dive down on us and the whole place shimmies. A muddy horse track wends in and out of the coaster tracks and along our pavilion. Bearing child riders, the blindered horses are led by stooped, old black men with slouch hats. As if mechanical, the horses neither shy nor even flinch as the cars hurtle by. Their passengers hold their hands high above their heads and shriek. I hate the noise, and each time the cars scream overhead I clamp my ears. I want terribly to ride one of those sad horses, but I am only five years old and not nearly tall enough. At the entrance to each ride stands a cardboard likeness of either Howdy Doody or Henry, from the *Little Lulu* comics. I measure up to Howdy Doody, but Henry has a head on me, and that's who you have to match to ride horses.

"Let's ride the Jackrabbit," Francene suggests.

"I don't want to."

"C'mon. It'll be fun." She takes me by the hand and we get in line.

"I don't want to."

"Why?"

"I just don't want to."

I am too ashamed to admit I am terrified. As I pass Henry, he looks down on me with practiced indifference. If a parent is with you, you can ride anything. The attendant fixes the belt across our thighs and brings down the panic bar. We inch out, then slowly chug up the first slope. Francene smiles. She wears a sundress and turquoise babushka.

From the pavilion come the familiar verses of "Maria." I look down. Angelina stands on a picnic table, leading everyone in the song. The horses clop by, their heads down, the black men's heads down. Higher we climb as if winched —*click, click*—the whitewashed timbers creaking until we reach the pinnacle. We pause for a moment, and I peer down and see directly beneath me the creases of the old

Italian men's fedoras as they drink whiskey and play Amore. Much further off, the steely, green water of the Monongahela swells the valley.

Were I not catatonic with fright, and secured by leather and steel, I would jump out right here. The height means nothing to me. Indeed this is what I am contemplating when the coaster plunges into the abyss. Unable to help it, I scream. I cry. But every sound I make is swallowed by my own heart and stomach and the racket of wood and steel laughing as I die.

At first, Francene doesn't notice. She glances at me, but must think I am delighted. I cannot catch my breath to speak or move my hands from the bar to clutch at her. Only after we are slowly trundling up the second slope she realizes, and puts her arms around me.

"I want to get off," I scream. I can't take another fall.

"We can't get off, honey."

Each time we climb I watch the same world below, Angelina singing and the old men throwing out their fists of gnarled fingers, the food spread over the tables, the horses at their laps like time winding down. Then we fall and the blurred world stuffs me with my own breathless screech. Finally the big lever is jerked and the cars creak to a stop. I can't stop heaving. Francene carries me back to the pavilion, and for some reason lays me in the fleshy, warm arms of Angelina. I am ashamed for crying in front of everyone.

"Why are you so upset, little one?" she asks.

"I just wanted to ride the horses. But I'm too little."

"You want to ride the horses, you ride the horses."

Still holding me she stands and walks over to the man at the entrance to the track. She tells him she is Angelina Colaizzi, a movie star who has traveled on a plane from Arizona to be there at Kennywood just for Italian Day, and that Henry or no Henry, he should put me up on whatever horse I want or she'll see about it.

The guy looks at her like "Big Deal," then ushers me to the front of the line and asks me what horse I want to ride. I choose a black-saddled, white horse, the only white one, splattered with mud and droppings. One of the black men lifts me up and then leads me slowly around the track. The horse doesn't seem to know I am there. He plods along with his head down as I clamp the saddlehorn with one hand and run my hand up and down his clipped bristly mane with the other, clucking and telling him he is a good boy. Francene and Angelina stand watching just on the other side of the corral, waving as I pass. Each time the rumbling shadow of the Jackrabbit bolts over me, I lean forward and pet the old white horse's neck.

When I am lifted down by the black man, Angelina is gone. Francene takes me back to the pavilion. We eat and watch a group dressed in peasant costumes dance the tarantella and perform an Italian quadrille while one of the old Amore players, very tipsy and very serious, plays the accordion. I am happy because of the horse, and the way it is getting dark; and I like the music and all the desserts.

After, we gather at the lake and watch fireworks. I cover my ears as a man is blown out of a cannon across the water and into a net. There is more dancing. Several men ask Francene to dance, but she refuses, sitting next to me on a bench and feeding me lemon ice Moio's Italian Pastry Shop has donated.

At the end of the night Father Vita appears on the stage of the amphitheater behind the lake and says a few words and a few prayers. Then the Holy Name Society, wearing striped sashes, carries out the life-sized statue of Santa Rocco. He looks a lot like Jesus, long dark hair and beard, except he wears a wide-brimmed hat, almost a cowboy hat, and lavish red robes and skirts. His left hand holds up the robe hem, revealing a grotesquely womanish right leg. In his right hand is a long staff with a little cross at the top and ribbons cascading down from it. He wears a striped sash, too. The men toting him step onto a flatboat lit with candles, and paddle him across the lake. Everyone claps and bravos, and the very old people cry and make Signs of the Cross. As a missionary, during the plague years in Italy, Santa Rocco ministered to the dying, and contracted the disease himself. Left to die in an abandoned building, a dog brought him bread, and he was cured. Thenceforth, accompanied by the dog, he traveled about curing people. He is good luck.

• • •

In my hand is a round, shiny white stone the size of a jelly bean. What we call a lucky stone. Francene and I are living in a row house on one-way Prince Street and I'm standing in an unkempt thicket of scraggly boxwood, wearing a cowboy shirt embroidered with lariat loops and stitched-on rhinestones. No grass grows in this tiny yard I am forbidden to leave. My sixth birthday is twelve days away.

A gray, four-door Ford rumbles by, and I heave the stone which strikes the car on the front fender. The car stops. I crouch down among the bushes. Slowly the car backs up the street and stops even with the thicket. There is a man and woman with a child between them in the front seat. In the rear are two more children and an old woman wearing a black feather hat sitting at the window closest to me. She is pointing at me, and yelling, "There he is. There's the little bastard." Her finger aimed at my heart is like a curse, so palpable it knocks me back off my haunches into the mud.

Then they are all pointing and yelling, "There he is." Even the children. They streak out of their car and, like a lynch mob, shove me up the two flights of concrete steps to our porch and beat on the door until Francene opens it. Barefoot, she wears a silky, flowered, belted robe. Her hair is tied on top of her head with a scarf and she holds a recently lit cigarette in the long red-nailed fingers of her right hand, like Bette Davis in *The Petrified Forest*, the same dusky filmic light framing her plaintively in the doorjamb.

"Is this your kid?" asks the old woman who is holding onto me.

"Yes he is and please take your hands off him," replies Francene.

Behind her in the next room come sounds like someone walking across the floor, ice clinking in a glass, a struck match, a door opening or closing. Francene turns toward it for a second before looking down at me and smiling, her teeth slightly bucked, her lipstick shiny. Joan Crawford's mouth.

"Do you know what he did?" asks the woman as she releases me.

"Tell her what he did," she commands the man, who stands on the top step with his wife and the three children.

"He must have robbed a bank," Francene murmurs.

"He hit our car with a rock," states the man.

"We could have wrecked," says his wife.

By the way the children look at me, I can tell they are thankful to not have my life.

"Well, I am terribly sorry, and I'll be sure to punish him," says Francene. "Did the rock do any damage to your car?"

"No," says the man.

"I'm not so sure," snaps the old woman.

"I'd like to pay you."

"No," replies the man, backing down the steps. "C'mon," he says to his wife and children.

"If you'll hold on a minute and let me get my purse."

"We don't want any money." He turns, followed by his family, and walks back down to the car parked at the curb.

The old woman stands there staring at Francene.

"I'd see that his father gave him a good licking."

"I'll do that," says Francene. Then she guides me into the house and, with the woman still on the porch, closes the door. We sit side by side on the couch and she asks why I threw the rock. I listen to whoever it is trying not to make noise in the next room. I tell her over and over that I don't know why.

"Who is that in there?" I ask.

"Why did you throw the rock?"

"Who is it?"

"Why in God's name would you throw a rock at a car?"

"I don't know."

"Do you want to end up in Juvenile Court?"

"I don't care."

I am so humiliated, I want to get sick and die. I want to hurt Francene with my pain and suffering. But all I manage to do is fall asleep. When I wake up I have another of my terrible side-aches, God's punishment for my hitting that car with the white stone. I lie in the dark and listen to the cars whoosh by, the strains of clarinet music coming from the Zitellis', hushed mechanical voices from another part of the house. Above my bed a wrought-iron sampler reads: *Now I lay me down to sleep. I pray the Lord my soul to keep. If I should die before I wake, I pray the Lord my soul to take.* Suddenly I'm terrified of dying, of the dark and the unbearable pain. But I know not to cry. Instead I call for Francene, and she instantly appears. She carries me into the living room and lays me on the couch. On the big black-and-white TV plays *Going My Way.*

From the cedar chest Francene lifts a square of thick yellow wool and places it on my side, under the waistband of my pajamas. She sits on the floor next to the couch, nuzzles her nose into my neck and sings "Tura Lura Lura" along with Bing Crosby as he serenades the dying old priest played by Barry Fitzgerald. When she comes away, my neck is wet, but she is smiling and I think the pain is easing up. But I don't want it to go away entirely. I want to be in it another moment more.

● ● ●

Francene lets me stay up late and watch old movies with her. She refers to them as good stories, and I sense they capture for her the essence of what she thinks her lost life has been about. For me they do the same. I develop a nostalgia for things I have never experienced, as if my existence is already memorialized in celluloid and I can never reenter it.

In my own life I do not always know what to feel, but I feel deeply what I see on screen. I simply can't get over William Bendix losing his leg in *Lifeboat*, or how those people fell upon the German sailor and threw him overboard. People are duplicitous like the townfolk in *High Noon*. Deranged like Charles Boyer in *Gaslight*. Unimaginably brave like Gunga Din.

These *are* good stories, and I view them as morality tales, like the Old Testament and Jesus's parables. Francene and I sit side by side on the couch, eating peanut clusters and nonpareils she has brought home from her job at the candy counter at Sears and Roebuck. Sometimes, like in *Mrs. Miniver* when the Luftwaffe bombs are shaking the pictures off the Minivers' walls, she holds my hand or digs her nails into my thigh, while balling Kleenex in her free hand and chain-smoking. She is elegant as Greer Garson, and I wish she'd call me "darling," but we never talk about our love for each other the way they do in the movies. Movie people aren't ashamed of their love. In *A Farewell to Arms*, Gary Cooper kneels at the deathbed of Helen Hayes and weeps openly until Francene leaves the room.

There are other movies I wish I hadn't seen, but from which I could not, God help me, turn away. *The Lodger*:

Jack the Ripper, clutching his black medical satchel, emerging from a shroud of London fog. Spencer Tracy as Jekyll and Hyde. Mrs. Danvers—statuelike in that flaming window as the house caves in in *Rebecca*. I stay up one night after Francene has fallen asleep on the couch beside me and watch *The Haunted Strangler* with Boris Karloff, an actor whose voice and looks give me chills. It is about an old gentleman who finds a scalpel behind a shelf of books. When he picks it up, he shapeshifts into a twisted, feral killer. I cannot rouse Francene from sleep, yet I refuse to turn off the TV. I sit there and watch the hideous movie like penance.

These images build a church in my head whose congregation is nightmare. At least one night a week I stagger in the dark from my bedroom to Francene's and crawl in beside her. "Say a few prayers," she says groggily, already asleep again. But if her door is shut, I am absolutely forbidden to enter—this is our one sacrosanct rule—even on those nights when my room fills with fog, out of which hunch slavering men in tuxedo shirts and black capes who mean to torture me. If her door is fastened I curl on the floor against it and don't make a sound, no matter what. Even if my nightmare has tracked me to her threshold, I have to stop there. Somebody is telling her he loves her. Clark Gable or Cary Grant, a good, honest man like my father. Like in the movies. I listen to their whispers until I fall asleep with my face against the door.

CHAPTER 2

———— • ————

We enter Sears and Roebuck through Lawn and Garden and take the escalator down to Sporting Goods. Poe, an eighth grader, two years older than I, walks ahead of me. He bobs cockily on his white hightops, past the locked rack of shotguns and hunting rifles, rods and reels and tackle, and a stainless steel tub of darting minnows, where the chubby, bald clerk with a Hitler mustache waits on a guy who whips a flyrod back and forth in his hand. They are both staring down into a glass case of lavish striped lures. Neither looks up as we pass.

We turn down the baseball aisle and try on a few gloves. I put my face against the rich oily leather and breathe. Poe takes a few swings with an Adirondack. In the rack is a black bat, a 31-inch Hillerich and Bradsby, Louisville Slugger with a white trademark in its middle and signed by Rocky Colavito. It shines like onyx and is so perfectly balanced and light that it cuts the air more like a blade than ash. What I envision standing there swinging it is how the white ball will sound leaping off its black sheen, its trajectory over the houses.

When Poe gets to the bin of baseballs, he looks all around. Over the top of the shelves, we see the tip of the rod the customer holds and hear traces of his discussion with the salesman about trout, wherever in the world one would fish for trout. Poe snatches a ball and stuffs it down the front of his pants. I have seen him do this dozens of times, and it seems foolproof. But it's wrong. Blatantly. And I know this, but it seems less wrong all the time, especially since I admire Poe in every way, and admire him no less for this. Even so, stealing is something I have promised Francene to never do again. Especially in this store where she works just one floor above. Francene has told me stories since I can remember about Juvenile Court, which I conceive of as a bit like hell. Where boys end up if they steal.

As we pass the bat rack on the way out I very deliberately grab the black bat and, without breaking stride, slip the knob end down the side of my dungarees, then slide it up under my T-shirt so that the barrel fits into my armpit, jam a hand into my pants pocket to grip it to my side, and leave by the same route we used to enter. I have sold my soul for one swing of that beautiful black bat.

● ● ●

My bicycle, a red American Racer, with two gears, a foot brake and a hand brake, is new, not brand new, but new to me. Francene bought it from Mrs. Zitelli, who decided to sell it when her son, Hugo, went away to seminary in Erie. Hugo was a tall, ascetic boy, always it seemed in his dead father's oversized white shirts and ties. An egghead, a sissy, a mama's boy, someone to be made fun of because of his unfortunate name, his fatherlessness (though I have no father), his physical clumsiness, and the fact that he dared stretch the limits of what was necessary to learn.

When the rest of the boys Hugo's age were playing ball, he slumped on his front porch in front of a chess board or practiced clarinet. He had a moustache by the time he was in eighth grade, and his only companion was a pet duck named Alfred, after the butler in *Batman*, that he received one Easter and miraculously kept alive after all the other ducklings and garishly dyed chicks had been handled to death by their little owners. That Mrs. Zitelli bragged constantly about him was a neighborhood joke. These are things I know about Hugo from afar. He was well older than I and, knowing he was a kind of pariah, I don't think I ever spoke a word to him. But I used to watch him as he served Mass, the way he would hold the paten to the communicant's throat, how he would light the altar candles, then snuff them out after the priest left the altar.

Everyone knew he wanted to be a priest, which is my secret desire, and this too branded him. The Zitellis' house sits behind us in the alley, and in the hot summer evenings, put to bed while it was still light, I would lie and listen

longingly through my open window to my nightly lullaby—
Hugo practicing his clarinet. Without fail, however,
Francene would barge into my room, shut the window and
rail against Hugo, that mama's boy, for keeping me awake.

What really happened to Mr. Zitelli, Hugo's father, is a
mystery. I don't really think he is dead; but *dead* is the word
people I know use when they are finished with something
or something is finished with them. As much as anything
it means silence and falsehood.

I can't imagine Hugo on this bike that now belongs to
me, a bike much finer than any ridden by the others riding
with me along Stanton Avenue toward the Caddy Grounds.

• • •

On Saturday nights during supper, Francene and I watch
Studio Wrestling on Channel 11. Good guys and bad guys
like Gorilla Monsoon, 600-pound Haystack Calhoun,
George Steele, Hurricane Bobby Hunt, Killer Kowalski,
Cowboy Billy Watts, Johnny De Fazio, the tagteam midgets
and a horde of forgettable others who run the ropes and
turnbuckles, slamming each other around the ring for an
hour, while Ringside Rosie, a maddog fan who occasionally
slithers through the ropes and beats on the villains with
her umbrella, hollers encouragement and insults.

The play-by-play is done by Guy Morgan, who changed
his name from Morgano, Francene says. Because of this,

she has no respect for him, and tells me she knew him when his father bootlegged down the Hollow. I go to school with his daughter, Cheryl. *Studio Wrestling*'s big sponsor is American Heating Company, and its spokesman is Pie Traynor, the Pirates' great Hall of Fame third baseman from the twenties and thirties. Pie seems pretty old, with a big head of white hair. "Who can?" he asks, and then answers with the rhyme, "Ameri-can."

Our favorite wrestler, of course, is Bruno Samartino, the heavyweight champ of the world who lives just across the river from us. During World War II, his hometown of Pizzoferrato, Italy, was occupied by the Nazis, and for over a year he lived in a hill cave with his family to escape death at their hands. Indeed he looks like a caveman, a jutting rocky brow over recessed eyes, and a long mashed nose, off of which sweat trickles like a spigot during his postmatch interviews, the huge gold championship belt buckled over his tights. The undisputed best of the good guys, he is all upper body, huge, hairy pecs and biceps, a neck like an anvil and a booming, nasal voice. I've never seen him lose or wrestle dirty. I've seen him in trouble, and ganged up on, but he always wins, inevitably squeezing his opponent into submission with his signature bearhug. Once, I even saw him lift the Haystack over his head, twirl and bodyslam him.

One night, when I am eight, as we are watching the midgets and laughing ourselves silly, Francene rushes across the living room and, just fooling around, grabs me in a full nelson. I twist out of it and headlock her. Effortlessly, just the way it is done by Samartino on TV, she picks me up—she is incredibly strong—and bodyslams me onto the couch. She is laughing and looking at me like, "C'mon," so I rush her. We lock up and jostle around the living room until finally I drop down on one knee, wrap her legs with my arms and tackle her—which is where I think it will end. She is still in her work clothes, a skirt and sweater, nylons, makeup. Her nails are painted; she is always fussy about them. But, still on her knees, she lunges at me, and suddenly we are rolling around trying to pin each other. I don't know what it is, but neither of us wants to give up. For my part, I am not willing to let Francene, a woman, get the best of me like this; and she clearly does not wish to surrender to me. It's as if she wants to show me something about herself that I can never know otherwise.

She snares me in a scissors that squeezes my guts out. She almost barks, "Submit, submit," the way it is done on TV. It hurts me, but makes me mad, too. No way am I going to submit. I twist in her locked legs and grab her in a hammerlock until she lets out a huge breath and says "Ooh." Now hurt herself, she is angry and comes at me with a flying mare. But I move. She hits the floor so hard the rabbit ears fall off the TV, and I pounce with an atomic drop.

After that, every Saturday night, at some point during *Studio Wrestling*, Francene and I square off and wrestle. Poised above me, her stockings in runs, sweater furzed with carpet lint, and sweat standing out on her powdered lips and forehead, she works her lipsticked mouth into a grimace and finally pins me, holding my wrists for a three-count against the floor. I can smell that sweat too, nothing like a man's, but almost sweet, like the wild onions shooting out of the last of the snow in the very early spring outfield. There is a little fear there too, enough that it almost scares me.

• • •

We live on the first floor of a brick duplex on Lincoln Avenue, one block from Pittsburgh Hospital where I was born and one block from Our Lady of the Help of Christians Church where I was baptized. Above us lives a retired cop named Cooney who gets drunk on the front porch we share and brandishes his old police revolver until the woman he lives with, Hattie, coaxes him back inside. One night he has a heart attack and dies out there because I put the eyes on him. An ambulance comes and hauls him off. Its red lights spray my bedroom with what looks like blood and fire.

Living so close to the church and the hospital, the refrains of my life are bells and sirens, hearses and ambulances, cassocks and caskets, the impenetrable black stone of silence and solitude. But they don't bother me. I feel as if I have imagined myself, like the only character in a long, strange movie. As I begin losing my baby teeth, instead of placing them under my pillow for my fairy Godmother, I take them out to the trolley tracks running past our house and lay them on the rails to be powdered.

During the week, Francene leaves the house early for work, and I am left alone to get myself up, dress, eat breakfast, and walk almost a mile to school. When I get home, I eat whatever I want and do homework. Until Francene arrives home on the 82 Lincoln trolley, I play baseball in the backyard. This consists mainly of beating a rubber ball off the wall and catching it over and over, or hitting the ball out of my hand and running the broken-brick bases I have set up.

In the evenings, after Francene and I have eaten suppers of chipped-ham sandwiches, spaghetti, salted cashews, bridge mix and red pistachios, I go to the cellar and pitch against a rough brick wall, take swings at a tennis ball I've rigged on a string from the copper ceiling pipes, and oil my glove. If there is still light, I beg Francene to come outside and pitch to me. She chases me around the bases in her tight tweed skirt and high heels.

I keep scrapbooks, baseball cards, ledgers filled with statistics, and fall asleep every night during the season with a transistor radio, under my pillow, tuned to the Pirates' game. My interest in baseball is not a child's interest and this worries Francene. Her life is punctuated by the metronomic beat, hour after hour, of a ball against the house wall, then its thwack into my glove. She feels I substitute baseball for religion—for God—and attributes my obsession to the fact that I do not have a father. But she is wrong. Baseball and God are the same to me. Besides, my mother almost never goes to church. Sunday is her only day off, and she's still asleep at noon when I get home from Mass. On the rare occasions she attends, she never goes to Communion. Never. Which troubles me, but I don't know how to ask why. Nor do I want to know.

I am a boy who has always said he will marry his mother, even past the age when I've realized I will not. Without ever having been told, I know that there is not much money in the house. My great desire is to be a big league baseball player. Then there will be money to buy whatever Francene and I want. With such wealth, I can even buy a father.

● ● ●

A bat has somehow gotten into our house. It is the size of a tea saucer and looks like wet vinyl. Francene and I are petrified. She has always told me that bats attack people and tangle themselves up in their hair. Trying to ward it off with our flailing arms, as it dives at our heads and tries to nest in our hair, we run screaming through the house, knocking over lamps and furniture.

Francene shoves me into my bed and covers me head to toe. Sobbing, and screaming, "Francene," I peek out as she tries to fight off the bat, which beats itself off the walls and ceiling and then at her head of long brown hair. It has teeth and claws; it seems to get bigger and bigger. The vilest, ugliest thing I can imagine, it means to carry Francene away. Frozen under the covers, there is nothing I can do but watch.

My father walks into the room. He wears a white shirt and his hair is tousled, as if he has just rolled out of a nap. His face is bemused, and for a moment he surveys the strange scene, as if not sure whether he is really awake or marooned in a dream, like he isn't sure whether he belongs here. Each time Francene waves at the bat, she gives a little cry.

Then she looks and sees my father. He reaches out and simply snatches the bat in one motion, then dashes it to the floor where it lies still like a laminated black mortuary fan. This is my only memory of my father. The white shirt. His hair. The black bat at his feet. I don't know if he is looking at me. I don't even know if he knows I am here, hidden under the bedclothes. Perhaps I am dreaming this. But I swear it is not a dream, though I never ask my mother about it, and I still expect my father to come back and reenact this rescue. To come back. Just once. Memory is a pimp. It sells off for its own comfort what is most precious. I don't trust it and I never will.

● ● ●

I steer my bicycle with one hand and in the other carry my glove with the black bat threaded through the heel strap.

In the hand I steer with I also grip a white bakery bag with the lunch I packed in it: a Velveeta cheese sandwich, a fried chicken leg, a French doughnut, and a corked brown beer bottle filled with grape juice. As we turn onto Stanton from Meadow, right in front of Monicos' house, I drop the bag and the whole thing smashes. The white bread and orange cheese soak in purple and sharded brown glass. I brake and look down at it for a moment, thinking there might be some way around the fact of what I see at my feet. I should clean it up, but I don't have the heart. I know it is silly, but everything goes out of me, like I have given up.

Mrs. Monico, a stout, huge-breasted woman who speaks in staccato broken English, sweeps the sidewalk in front of her house. She calls to me. Tenderly it seems. But I am afraid of her. Francene says she puts the eyes on people. She might have put the eyes on me. The lunch fell because she cursed me. Cursed me because she has seen into my black heart. My black heart, black because of the theft of the black bat. Francene, the nuns, the world I live in, teach that you are called to answer for every trespass, small and large. They point to the wheelchaired cripple, the drunken vagrant, the cleft palate, the amputee, and fashion out of their miseries parables of comeuppance. Step out of line, and something bad happens to you. One way or another.

We ride to the Caddy Grounds, a baseball field that got its name because it was once part of a golf course. Its appeal is that it is in Highland Park, well out of our cement neighborhood of grassless, oiled public high school lots like Peabody Field. Not far in miles or even so much in blocks, but like forever, in the pastoral idylls of the well-to-do. The Caddy Grounds has grass in its outfield and real bases instead of rocks or squares of cardboard. To get there we pedal along Stanton Avenue, watching the row houses gradually burgeon into homes with plexiglass handrails, turrets, gables and enormous sod lawns with sprinkler systems and lawn jockies.

The nuns habitually lecture that good works are bricks and mortar, lumber, nails and shingles that you send up to God. Your heavenly dwelling is dependent on the quantity and quality of those materials. You may live in a castle or a shack. It is up to you. The people, living in those houses on the way to the Caddy Grounds, are already in heaven.

At the entrance to the park, on either side of the road, mounted on huge one-story block plinths, loom great bronze statues gone green with age and elements: stallions rearing, beside each of which is a vaguely nude, winged woman with long, flowing hair, and strapped with a broadsword, quiver and bow.

The boys I am with are older than me. I am not one of them, but I can play head to head with any of them. I slide when I have to, dive when I have to, and I never lift my head on a ground ball, even on a bad field. Above all, I never cry. Whenever I have occasion to, Francene swoops down on me and says, "Dry them up, Sad Sack." She holds me, she loves me, but she practically forbids my crying. She never cries. But she can be frantic, running a hand through her fringed brown hair that sits back off her face like a scarf, and smoking Kent after Kent, leaving the lipstick-stained filters, the same color as her pistachio-stained fingers, stumped out in piles in the chrome ashtray on the kitchen table. Francene and I are by ourselves. We aren't supposed to cry. This suits me, though I don't quite understand it. There is something she holds in, but it isn't the same thing I hold in. At least I don't think it is.

East Liberty

Chapter 3

There was a time when I was little, when Nonno was alive, when I stayed with Nonna while Francene worked. Before she had the job at Sears. Sometimes just for the day. Other times for longer periods when Francene was somewhere else working. Nonna has no hair and always has a black kerchief skinned around her head. Her only English is a patois laced with Italian, most of which I understand in context; but she never speaks to me except to tell me what to do, and I am afraid of her. In the dugout, frigid, rock basement is the steamer trunk that accompanied her from Naples. She tells me it is filled with the bones of her ancestors, and that if I ever attempt to open it a *scheletro* hand will reach out and drag me in and then I will be bones too. *Osso.* The bathroom is in the cellar, and on the nights I sleep in my grandparents' house I have to suffer a bath at the hands of Nonna.

Sitting there freezing in the two inches of water she allows, I close my eyes in shame as she scrubs my nakedness with pumice and a blue wedge of homemade soap. Then, in case I have to make *pisciare* in the middle of the night, I carry my bucket to the bedroom where I sleep, two floors above, that once belonged to Francene's only sibling, Uncle John, killed in Italy during the war. Francene excuses her parents, and their half century of arranged marriage, because of her brother's death. They have never been the same. Francene and Nonna do not get along. No one has ever told me, and I never ask, but I know it is something about my father. Everything would have been better, Francene tells me, had John lived. It was at the news of his death that Nonna's hair fell out.

I love my uncle's room, and when I awake I huddle in the big bed, the sun sluicing in through the stripped mottled branches of the sycamore as it scratches against the window. Facing me in a niche on the opposite wall is the portrait of Uncle John in his dress uniform. In one corner of the frame is the holy card—Jesus defying Satan in the desert, seraphim hovering at the borders—with his death date, December 18, 1944; the 23rd Psalm; and "DeRosa's Funeral Home" printed on the back; in another corner a lock of his black hair. Next to it rest a casket of service medals, the flag that had draped his coffin on the day of the funeral folded into a triangle, and streamers of Easter palm.

On Sundays and Holy Days of Obligation a lit votive candle flickers on the table in front of it. One morning, while it is still black dawn, on The Feast of the Assumption, I wake to a monster at the foot of the bed. Half man, half woman, it wears a long white gown and smells of garlic and mothballs. Flame spumes out of its bony hand. Its head is a giant cracked egg with bituminous brows and gold studs launched through cavernous ears. It is Spacaluccio, the *mostro* of night-becoming-day, who lives beneath the Hollow bridge and kidnaps bad children. Too paralyzed to scream, I lay perfectly still as the monster lights my uncle's votive, and I see his young, handsome face illuminated, pleased. And then the monster, my bald Nonna, I realize, kisses him and floats out of the room.

From his promontory, Uncle John looks as perfect and invulnerable as a movie star. Burt Lancaster. John Garfield. Any of them. And that's really how I conceive of him. An icon face stalled in time, never aging, never drawing back from anything. Under his eye I sit at his enormous oak desk and play with the T-square, compass, and protractor still situated perfectly on the blotter. He planned to be an engineer. In the drawers are old letters, high school yearbooks, a framed picture of the blonde, corsaged girl he left behind, and a letter opener, the size of a dagger, with a hilt and a leather scabbard. Vaunting it, I charge the room, careful of noise. I have strict orders to stay out of the desk, but I can't keep my hands off the letter opener, which I want badly.

Downstairs Nonna broods at the kitchen table, drinking hot water, chewing parsley and garlic, that black rag on her head, the Italian newspapers spread out in front of her. I go to her as instructed by Francene, kiss her gray cheek, and say, "*Bongiorno, Nonna.*"

"*Bongiorno, Roberto.*" She pats my cheek. Her breath is overpowering. Nonno is nowhere to be seen, but I smell him: anisette, strong coffee, diNobili cigars. A tailor from Naples, he almost never speaks. His jaw, shaped like a goblet, has rusted shut. Or the effort is too much. He barely opens it to eat, and his eyebrows have grown over his eyes. Nonna is always angry with him, so he stays gone from the house.

Silently I eat my breakfast of pastina and egg, and coffee loaded with milk and sugar. I leave the house as soon as I can. On Nonna's street, Omega Street, I discover baseball among the cracked concrete, glass and twisted metal. My first glove, waterlogged and unstrung, I find the summer between first and second grades on the roof of Goodwin's garages. I use a cracked bat, nailed back together, and balls I retrieve from the sewer, down to the yarn, wound with electrical tape. All day I play in the parched weedlot between the garages where Goodwin parks his trucks across the street from Nonna's house. There I learn to throw and bat and master the mystery of catching.

My only playmates are the Hilliard children, of whom Nonna disapproves greatly because they are black and

Protestant. She has a word for them in Italian, *tizzone*, that my mother tells me never to repeat. She also calls them *melanzano* because they are the color of eggplant. In winter I do not so much as catch a glimpse of them, but in the other seasons they are all over the street. How many there are I cannot rightly tell, nor am I always sure of their gender, except for those who wear dresses. Their mother sits on the porch and summons them with shrieks. I'm unable to determine a father, but the eldest male, very tall and Ethiopian, is Montmorrissey who wears earrings and scarves and sometimes women's wigs and high heels. He speaks in a woman's voice, carries a purse, and staggers late at night when he trips home to his mother's piercing summons. He has been to Juvenile Court. *Sudicio*, Nonna calls him. Filthy.

The Hilliards fear Nonna. They think she is a witch, all dressed in black and mumbling prayers and spitting parsley as she pitches along Omega Street on her way to church or to the huckster Fio's red truck from which Francene buys cigarettes while trying to ignore his crudity. As Nonna passes the Hilliards, without looking up, they whisper to themselves, "Mussolini," their nickname for her, but more like an antidote for whatever spell she casts upon them. The instant I come in from playing with them, I am remanded to the cellar for my bath. Nonna regards dirt with the same recoil with which a soul regards sin. If she could, she would boil me, and herself as well. She boils everything else. Clothes, plates, silverware, her eyeglasses and rosaries. There is always a cast-iron kettle of water boiling on the stove. She mops with it, swabs the sink and tables and counters with it. On hands and knees with a wire brush, she even scrubs her porch and sidewalk in front of the house.

No matter where she is at twelve noon, when the Angelus bells ring, she drops to her knees and prays, ending with a keening sob for her lost son. If I am with her at this hour, which I try to avoid, I must kneel too and pound my chest along with her.

I accompany her, carrying like a pack animal a bucket of tools, and a flat of flowers, on her trips by streetcar to the cemetery at Mount Carmel to care for my uncle's grave. When we first arrive she forces me to my knees, then throws herself on the grave. After a while she rises and sends me with the bucket for water so she can scour the stone. We then plant the flat of flowers, usually begonias or geraniums, and water them. Before we leave we say a rosary and she kisses and caresses and mumbles endearments to the stone. On the way out of the cemetery, Nonna and I fill a pillowcase with *ciccoria* we spade up from the still fallow graveland, to take home for *ensalada*.

On Good Friday she ties sheets over the windows and mirrors, turns off all the lights, and by candlelight, from noon to three, we make sausage, while on the stove in a bubbling cauldron the pig's head with which to break the

Lenten fast turns side to side in the roil of its own liquor. Not one word is permitted. Absolute *silenzio*. My job is to mix with my bare hands in a huge tub lean pork, fat meat, garlic, salt, black pepper, eggs, bread crumbs and the pig's blood. Nonna douses the whole thing with holy water and then returns to the sink to scrub one more time the intestines which we will use for the casings.

Literally up to my elbows, kneading and beating, the splashing eggs and blood slippery and turning orange as they mix among the pinkish-brown meat, the smell carnal and gamey, I close my eyes and gag until it is finished. After the intestines are scissored into lengths and tied off at one end, I blow into the open end until it swells like a balloon, and hold it open while Nonna spoons in the mixture, then ties off the other end. Even though she will scrub my hands and arms, using a toothpick to dig the swine out from under my fingernails, finally sterilizing me with near- boiling water, they will remain stained and seared for a week and then develop a rash from the pig. At three o'clock, the hour of the savior's death, she falls facedown spreadeagled on the kitchen floor and weeps.

Francene and I eat Easter dinner at my grandparents' house. In the middle of the laden table is the pig's head, crowned with sprigs of rosemary, raspberries and apple, the tongue and brains on separate serving platters. Nonno is animated. All day he has spent drinking and playing bocci with his *paisans*.

He refuses to remove his fedora. His droopy gray mustaches drip *vino* onto his vest. A pitcher of red wine sits within his reach. He pours a glass and puts it in front of me.

"Papa," Francene says, smiling.

"Luigi," Nonna hisses at Nonno. "*Aspettera.*" Wait.

She makes the Sign of the Cross, as do we all, and dips her black-sheathed head to her folded knuckly hands. Her invocation is protracted and in dialect. It is like the rest of us are not there. Nonno drinks wine during the prayer. Francene stares at her mother. The pig stares at me.

"*Mangiare,*" eat, orders Nonna when she tearily concludes, then begins ladling *minestra* into the soup bowls.

I lift my glass of wine. "*Saluto,*" I say as I've heard Nonno say before he drinks.

He and my mother laugh. Even Nonna smiles though she is looking not at me, but at Nonno. He takes up his glass. "*Saluto,*" he says, then drains it. I take a sip of the bitter wine and choke a bit, but I get it down. I do not want to disappoint him. The pig looks at me through gray, marbled, oily eyes. Its left ear hangs.

"*Mangiare,*" says Nonno. Taking his spoon, he scoops out one of the pig's eyes and swallows it. He digs out the other and plops it on my plate. "*Buona fortuna.*"

I look at Francene.

"For good luck," she says.

The jellied eye fixes me in its curse. Nonno rips an ear

from the pig, which, with its eyes gouged out, looks bewildered and sacrificial.

"*Mangiare*," mumbles Nonno as he gnashes the ear. He spears the eye on my plate with his fork and holds it to my mouth.

"*Mangiare*," he repeats.

The tips of his moustaches coagulate. I open my mouth and swallow whole the eye, then drain my glass of wine. Inside me now it sees everything.

"*Bravo*," laughs Nonno, and fills my empty glass.

"No, Papa," chides Francene.

Nonna launches into a tirade in Italian. She stabs her knife toward him and says that she does not want him to make of me a drunkard like him. He laughs and makes a noise mocking Francene and Nonna, then seizes the empty pitcher to replenish it from his barrels in the cellar. At the top of the stairs he trips and we hear him bang down the splintery planks until his final crash and oath, the pitcher exploding, when he hits the rock wall. He is crumpled against the wall, his hat still clamped on his head and blood falling out of it. Francene runs to him.

Ubriaco. Drunkard. Leave him, Nonna tells her and returns to the table. The wine is in my head and the pig in my stomach. I am not sure who I am.

• • •

Chasing a ball into the street I am almost run over by a car. One of the Hilliard girls bangs on Nonna's door and tells her. By my ear, Nonna leads me down to the cellar, sits me in an old ladderback chair and ties me to it with clothesline. The only light sprays in the opened cellar window through which I hear the other children playing, punctuated occasionally by Mrs. Hilliard's shrills.

Maybe Nonna loves me—that she would punish me for almost getting run over. Still I do not like being stuck in the chair in the damp, dark cellar with its trunk of bones. There is a bat in the house, and it has a face. It chases us from room to room. It wants Francene, her long hair, parted on the side, like Lauren Bacall's in *To Have and Have Not*. The bat will nest in Francene's hair, and she will die if I cannot stop it. But I cannot stop it. I am just a boy. Francene screams and beats at her head as the bat burrows into her beautiful hair, its awful face against hers.

I am calling for my father, but having never known a father—what is the endearment for a father one has never known?—I have no name for him, but I call nonetheless because he will come as he does in my memory and kill the bat, but he does not come. This time my father does not come, the bat attacking Francene, and she screaming with her hands in her long brown hair, and I have no word either for my terror or the weight of sorrow crushing me.

When I wake, trussed in the cellar chair, I am in the

grip of a rending side-ache. I am alone so I cry. There seems so much to cry about, so little to cry about, the difference being exactly the same. I want Francene, but I do not know when she will be back for me. The pain is past much, but I decide I will hold out for her. I pray, but to no avail. Finally when I can stand it no more, I shriek for Nonna.

She unties me, but I cannot straighten myself for the pain. She half carries, half drags me up the stairs to the living room couch. I drink the hot concoction of lemon, honey, and elderberry brandy she gives me, submit to the crucifix she tapes over my paining side. She brings me a clove of garlic.

"*Mangiare*," she says.

I turn my head. The pain is so much.

"*Mangiare*."

The smell of her alone is enough garlic. I keep my face pressed to the green brocade of the couch, to the sound of the Hilliards playing baseball in Goodwin's lot across the street. Nonna, eyes closed, sits across the room, saying Hail Marys on her wedding rosary:

> *Dio ti salvi, Maria, piena di grazia;*
> *il signore e teco; tu sei benedetta fra*
> *le donne e benedetto e il frutto del*
> *ventre tuo, Gesu.*
> *Santa Maria Madre di Dio, prega per noi*
> *peccatori adesso e nell' ora della nostra morte.*

I lift my swimming head and see at the door my bat and swollen glove admonishing me for having cried. They exaggerate my sorrow. When I wake this time Francene kneels at my side, her cool soft hand on my forehead. The pain is gone.

• • •

I want to tell the Hilliards that I have been tied up, that I wasn't really scared in the cellar. I feel gratitude toward the girl who cared so much that I might have been run over by a car that she tattled on me. I also feel anger. Vendetta. But I say nothing. I hit the ball on lines that steadily rise over the outstretched arms of everyone and roll into the weeds all the way to Ryder Street from which I can see the nuns planting flowers in the convent yard. I leap up and, like a magician, produce in my glove balls that have already disappeared. Then I throw them the length of the lot to stop runners at home plate. The Hilliards tell me I am good, and I feel for the first time welcomed by them. Powerful in some new way so that when the game ends I do not go back to Nonna's where Francene waits for me.

Instead I follow them deeper into the weeds and Goodwin's barbed wire jungle of rusted discarded machinery. Raymond Hilliard pulls out matches and starts a fire with dead burdock and cardboard. We feed it twigs and jagged rotting lumber with nails spiking out. Bigger and bigger pieces until the fire is trembling. The Hilliard boys take their shirts off and dance around it, poking it with sticks and throwing rocks in it. Sparks shoot up and die among the telephone wires.

We square off with rocks and sail them at one another, taking shelter behind piles of railroad ties and ingots. Rocks bash off the moldy plywood I crouch behind with Terry Hilliard. We look at each other and laugh, count 1-2-3, then charge up and ambush Piggy Hilliard who is out in the open in front of the flames, now as tall as he. He undulates in the shimmering heat, his fat belly hanging over undershorts peeking up from his pants, his girlish breasts like Jell-O as he throws rocks back at us. Then he disappears in the smoke as Terry and I dive for cover, rocks tattooing the plywood. One of them hits behind us with a ping and ricochets into the back of my head. This strikes me as terribly funny, and I continue throwing as I laugh until I see in Terry's face something wrong and feel the warm scarf of blood on my bare neck. When I put my hand to my head it comes away dripping scarlet, and I take off running for Nonna's.

I suppose I scream the whole time I run, the Hilliards on my tail as I careen along Omega Street. Mrs. Hilliard comes out of the house and tries to corral me. Even Montmorrissey, mincing home with his brown bag, attempts to help. But, terrified by the blood, I dodge them all, Nonna and Francene out on the porch and heading toward me. Assuming the entire Hilliard family is chasing me in order to finish off the job they have started by bloodying my head, Francene scoops me up and screams, "Leave him alone. You leave him alone. What have you done to him?" Nonna, waving a coal poker, hurtles into their midst, shrieking, "*Animales*" and the other Italian words of derogation. The entire Hilliard family scatters, including Mrs. Hilliard who yells, "You're crazy." Montmorrissey, walking backwards and lifting his bottle every few seconds to Nonna, drinks and lets loose with long coughs of laughter.

Inside, Francene and Nonna sift through my hair and find the tiny hole. Nonna forces a big Italian coin down on the lump to suppress the swelling. Then she takes a wad of black Wooly Salve, sticks it to the cut and fastens it with tiny crisscrossed strips of white adhesive. I try to explain that it was an accident, that the Hilliards are my friends, but by now the sirens are slicing through the house, and when we go to the window we see thick black smoke and geysers of flame shooting over Goodwin's garage.

All of Omega Street gathers to watch the firemen fight the fire which consumes mainly trash and weeds and one of Goodwin's trucks. I do not even chance a look at the Hilliards. With my bandaged head and sidled against Francene, I keep silent. It is worth a split head to have her back, to be able to go home again with her.

"Kiss Nonna good-bye," she tells me. Nonno is not there.

I go to Nonna and kiss her dry cheek. "Good-bye, Nonna."

She pats my cheeks and kisses me on the mouth with her wrinkled garlic lips. "*Ciao, Roberto.*"

"I forgot my baseball," I say and race upstairs to Uncle John's room. In the middle of the bed is the black-taped ball. I pick it up, go to the desk, remove the letter opener and scabbard, lift my pantleg and slip it into my sock. My uncle looks down at me and remains untroubled.

On the way home, Francene and I stop at Isaly's and buy chipped ham, sauerkraut, pickles and Klondikes for our supper in front of television. The movie is *The Stratton Story*, a true story about a baseball player, a pitcher named Monty Stratton, played by James Stewart, who shoots himself in a hunting accident and has to have his leg amputated. At first he gives up and feels sorry for himself, but his wife, June Allyson, never loses hope and because of her love and support he ends up getting an artificial leg and making a comeback.

But it is wrenching to watch him out on the mound for his first game back, teetering on the prosthetic leg, falling on his face, his wife with her hand to her face, Francene with her hand to her face.

EAST LIBERTY

CHAPTER 4

———●———

Christmas Eve, 1960. I am waiting for Francene. She will bring a tree and we will decorate it as a Christmas gift for my grandparents. Nonna is busy with the fish. On the stove the sauce bubbles, calamari, little black-horned octopi, swimming at the top. The baccala, like a baseball bat, spans the kitchen counter. Nonna washes scungilli and eel, unhinges clams with a knife and drops them in the sink to soak. The kitchen smells like the fishmonger's. There is nothing to do. The Hilliards do not come out in the winter, and my grandparents refuse to own a television.

I come down from Uncle John's room where I have been jumping on his bed and sit at one end of the kitchen table to make with paste and scissors a garland of colored paper for the tree. At the other end is the flattened and floured pasta dough, cut into strips for fettucine. Nonna takes another tray of pasta upstairs to spread on one of the beds and cover with a sheet to dry. From upstairs comes a profound oath and conjure, followed by a swooning cry like the ones I've heard when she is lamenting Uncle John. I run to the bottom of the stairs and there she is on top of the landing, a black triangle, holding in her hands torn ribbons of dough I have unwittingly massacred.

Descending one step at a time. "*Stupido.*" Like a giant puppet being lowered by stage wires. "*Stupidaggine.*" As if she will fling herself from above and smother me. "*Stupido,*" over and over until I can't stand it, because I know it is true, and run out the door into the snow.

Without my coat, I wander as long as I can stand the cold, until I am lost, the driving snow and pitch night disorienting me. I trip on freezing feet down an alley of falling-in abandoned houses. In the one I choose for shelter there are gypsies who warm themselves and toast apples over coffee cans in which they have kindled fires. Nonna says they are *diavolos*, but I believe them devout people. I see them in church, sipping holy water out of the fonts. I wish to ask their forgiveness for the breach in my family I have caused with my birth. They offer me an apple at the end of a stick, but when they smile their faces in the firelight collapse into oily dough. I run out the way I came in and in so doing step on a nail jutting up through a piece of wood that goes through my tennis shoe and into my foot. I keep running nonetheless, the wood flapping in the snow.

I smell bread from Stagno's Bakery and suddenly I see where I am. On a bluff on the white side of Negley Run, its streetlights whirling in the snow, the Hollow bridge looms, half visible. Directly across from me on the other side of the boulevard is another bluff upon which the black projects perch, one atop the other, like giant toy blocks. The gulf between the promontories through which the boulevard gashes is the demilitarized zone for East Liberty's cherished race wars: the Hollow. The Italian word for it, like all Italian words, comes from the tongue and not from the dictionary. *Buh-sha-wa-lone.* I can only mimic the word; I cannot spell it. With the accent like a sledgehammer on the first syllable: *Buh-sha-wa-lone.* The forbidden place. Nonna crosses herself when she says it. It remains East Liberty's last pittance of wilderness, a few unclaimed acres in the heart of the neighborhood.

To me it is a country, a hilly jungle of trees and vines, a stream and rock outcroppings, filled with a century of trash and the amnesiac dispossessed, not clearly alive, ambling like the citizens of Limbo. *Diavolos.* In the spell of Spacaluccio, my grandmother's conjure, even now gaping from his nap and scratching his horned head against the concrete bridge abutment, shivering the entire looming structure, gypsies falling from their homes in the spans like angels out of heaven.

• • •

A few times a year I enter the Hollow with the older boys, carrying knives and matches, leaving the trails and switchbacks to fan through the beggar lice and crabapple stands, avoiding the wandering mumblers and sick gypsies, on the lookout always for a similar party of black boys from the projects. High in the trees are abandoned treehouses with filthy words carved into them, charred magazines of naked women, used rubbers we call Allegheny whitefish. Even an escaped monkey from the zoo, but no one has ever seen it.

There is all manner of refuse. Entire libraries, suits of clothes, the roof from a house, a life-size statue of Saint Anthony, a crate of desiccated gas masks. Everything in varying states of decay. We hike beyond the bridge—I get dizzy just walking under it—until we reach the stream at the verge of Washington Boulevard in the deepest woods where the Allegheny River feeds it green water. Then we strip and streak ourselves with mud and mine the water for crayfish—we call them crabs—and the black slimy newts— mud puppies—turning over every rock in the creek bed until we have a discarded pink bathtub slopping over with them and are ready for the Inquisition.

With matches and knives and sharpened sticks we build our bloody little holocaust with those utterly strange little creatures who don't seem to mind at all. How fascinating to watch a writhing, skewered newt shrivel over a slow flame, or the beheaded crayfish still push ahead of him the stick jammed in his pincers.

It is there amidst this slaughter that I learn from Poe

the story of men and women. He grins, letting the cigarette smoke waft out of his mouth, then sucking it back in through his nostrils. A French inhale. He wears sunglasses. I see his broken tooth flash in a narrow shaft of sunlight knifing through the sumac. Even though he has the pictures to prove what he claims, it seems to me an unlikely explanation, and I refuse to believe him, though I know he must be right. It can only be something this taboo.

A black snake, the length and width of a pencil, with a yellow ring around its head, wriggles through the grass next to Poe. It is the first snake I have ever seen outside of the zoo. Then it strikes me that I have seen a real snake once before, though I can't be sure I haven't dreamt it. A snake I stumbled upon somewhere, I don't remember where, when I was a baby. I had only begun talking. When I saw the snake I cried out and a man—I took him for my father—came and beat the snake to death, then looped it over a stick and held it up in front of me where I could study the mosaic of its skin, the glassy detachment of its eyes.

With this memory comes also a remembrance of an unclothed woman—Francene?—strolling out of the bathroom and walking down the hall and stepping over me—I had been playing on the linoleum floor with a ball—and then the door closing and the voice of the man who killed the snake. I sit patiently with the ball outside the door until I hear the bell from Pete's ice cream truck outside, and take off running for the front door. A chair leg trips me and I go down on my face. The carpet is incarnadine, great funereal roses swirling about me. Pete's bell trills gaily, but I cannot get up. Knowing no better than to cry, I wail loudly until I am lifted from the floor, blood dripping into the carpet like ellipses as I am carried to the kitchen by a woman who turns out to be Francene. She wears a white slip adorned with tearoses of blood.

• • •

Poe picks up the snake and holds it in his cupped hands. The creature coils and raises its head, the tongue jabbing in and out. I don't want Poe to kill it, yet I say nothing. He lets it slide out of his hands back into the grass where it quickly disappears.

The pictures, though. I can't take my eyes off of them. The men and the women in them. They sap me of something dear, something that I need to keep things from getting too close. What Poe says is true. But it shouldn't be. Not for me. Not yet. My name is guilt.

To prove myself, Poe says, I must be initiated. Naked I stand among them, naked too. They lay me on a big flat rock. Poe slips out his bloody knife and puts the blade against my still hairless penis. Feeling the blade cold against me, I close my eyes and look up at the sky on the inside of my eyelids.

• • •

At the thought of Spacaluccio I know what I must do to placate Nonna. I will go to the Hollow bridge and find him and kill him with Uncle John's letter opener. Or he will eat me and that will be my judgment. I will offer myself to him like a Christmas fish. Either way. But first I must pry off the board fastened to my foot. My feet are so numb I feel the nail pulling out only as one feels a fingernail being clipped off. My hands, jammed in my pockets, are near useless. The snowclouds mute all light, but I travel by the boulevard lamps and the glow they impart to the snow, the bridge getting bigger, filling the sky as I walk, on its back cars with tiny headlights snailing along.

I have never been to the Hollow at night. On the dirt slopes beneath the bridge, gypsies drink wine and sing the old Italian Christmas songs. I unsheathe the letter opener. Directly above me is the underbelly of the bridge and its coiling superstructure like a giant ladder that I suddenly wish to climb. To be able to stand on the top and look out over my own life. And then fly away from it. Way up there surely would be angels. I am so cold.

"Spacaluccio," I call and the night calls back,

"Spacaluccio," again and again, as the gypsies laugh and call, "*Buon Natale.*" Then I feel his furnace breath on the back of my neck and glimpse astonishment in the creature eyes of the bridge gypsies. His shadow grows larger until it subsumes mine, the broad brim of horns fanning out from his head. Smelling the banked coals of his intestines, I turn and slash with the letter opener.

It is Nonno, looking down upon me, his hat flaked with snow, his mustaches frosted, a fire-tipped diNobili stabbing out of them. Not saying a word, he puts the hat on my head, takes off his overcoat and wraps me in it, then holding my hand leads me back to my grandparents' house.

Nonna stands on the porch, her hands steepled together. She cries and kisses me, jabbers in Italian, calls me *bambino*. I throw my arms around her and allow myself to be led upstairs and changed into warm clothes. "*Benedire*," she says and strokes my cheeks like I am hers. Calls me her lamb. *Agnello*.

As we wait for Francene I sit wrapped in a blanket with a red hot water bottle at the table with Nonno. He drinks wine and cracks roasted hazelnuts for me. I drink coffee with milk and sugar and anisette. Nonna sets the table and begins putting out the food. She unwraps the one Christmas ornament they brought from Italy: the angel Gabriel holding in each hand a candle which she places in the middle of the table with a sprig of holly. Nonno lights a wooden kitchen match, hands it to me and I light the candles.

"*Saluto*," says Nonno and drinks.

"*Saluto*," I say and lift my bowl of coffee.

"*Buono Natale*," says Nonna, turning off the kitchen lamps so that the little blue and gold angel from Naples wields the only light.

I am not sure whether to be sad or happy. I like this light that makes the room a church, the way it twinkles off the glasses and cutlery, softening everything, snow sifting down. I miss Francene. I am worried about her. But my grandparents are so seemingly content, even happy, that I feel for the first time I belong here—with them. They must know something wonderful is about to happen. Francene is going to surprise us with something. She is late because she is bringing home my father.

We wait. Nonna drops the trampled fettucine into boiling water. Nonno drinks more wine until he is a stone at the end of the table. Their faces begin to metamorphose and gray in the flicker. *Francesca.* Nonna keeps talking about Francene. Where is she? Why so late? Where? Where? *Dove?*

I want to say something on her behalf. If only she would come now, then everything would be all right. When we can wait no longer, Nonna says, "We eat," and my grandfather nods like yes and no, who cares? I am sleepy from the anisette and full of hazelnuts. I merely move the buttered fettucine around my plate. I refuse to eat the fish sauce.

"*Mangiare,*" says Nonna, her face suddenly drained. She eats, but hardly at all.

Nonno with his fork twirls the pasta against his soup spoon, the calamari intertwined, and hoists them to his hairy mouth. As he chews, the horns twist over his pink bottom lip. Baby octopi. It makes me sick to look at them, flopped in the bowl of fettucine, the roasted red peppers and green olives diced in the baccala, mushroom caps stuffed with crabmeat, the blackly pellucid eel I expect to be electrocuted by. He crunches through the smelts, bone and all. He takes up his purple glass and breaks off another piece of bread. His mustaches are fish.

Francene, smiling, her hair wavy and radiant with snow, bursts in the door with a Christmas tree. I jump up and run to her, and she almost loses the Christmas tree hugging me. She leans it against the door and walks into the kitchen.

"Francesca," says my grandfather, "*Buono Natale*."

"*Buono Natale*, Papa."

They kiss. Francene no longer smiles. She not only knows something is up, she knows what it is. A sequel to something that started long ago. Not just today.

Nonna has not lifted her head from the plate since Francene walked in. She is deciding how to react, struggling with some old thing rooted in blood that blackmails her into declaring ruination. I can almost hear it grinding in her as she purses her mouth and folds and unfolds her hands in her lap. Francene kisses her.

"*Buono Natale*, Mama."

Nonna tries to answer, but there is that root in her that cannot be dislodged.

"I'm sorry I'm late. I got the tree."

Nonno, with the fish mustaches, is a stone. Francene

has brought home a tree instead of my father. Or maybe I am the son of a tree. But I cannot ask Francene about my father. I learn that night that I must never ask her. That I don't want to know.

"I'm sorry, Mama."

One of my Nonna's hands claws its way to the tabletop. She lifts her face to look at Francene.

"Late? Late? You . . ." But she doesn't finish. The color has all come back to her face with a hiss.

"What?" snarls Francene. "What am I? Say whatever it is." Her hair and coat glisten with melting snow. "Let's go, Bobby. Get your things," she says to me.

I look at Nonna and Nonno, then get my bag. Francene and Nonna stare at each other. Then Nonna gets up, goes to the counter, gathers a hand of the uncooked, ruined fettucine and shakes it in Francene's face.

"What's that supposed to mean? Is that some kind of curse?" Francene laughs, like clearing her throat.

Nonna throws down the pasta, then goes over to the counter and sweeps the rest to the floor.

"Jesus Christ," says Francene. "C'mon, Bobby."

Out the door into the night. I don't even say good-bye to my grandparents. A few paces down Omega Street we hear the door open and we turn. Nonna walks out of the house carrying the Christmas tree Francene brought. She throws it into the street.

"Merry Christmas," says Francene, grabbing my hand and almost trotting through the snow. My foot from the nail hurts badly. As we pass the Hilliards', I see them through the window, singing and having a good time, Montmorrissey dancing with Mrs. Hilliard.

Francene doesn't seem to know what to do. We are both cold and have a long way to go. I don't even know if she has any money. At first I hope we might go back to my grandparents' or one of them would come after us and insist we return. But there is never any going back. It's my fault. I tell Francene about ruining the pasta.

She laughs. "At least I know why she was throwing macaroni on the floor. That was a new one."

"I'm sorry."

"You didn't do anything. It had nothing to do with you."

I can hardly walk. I try not to limp. My tennis shoes are sopping from the snow. If I tell Francene about the nail, she'll take me to Pittsburgh Hospital for a tetanus shot. I had to get one when the Hunters' dog bit me. We waited for hours in the dim-lit marble hall on a long bench next to orange and blue oxygen cylinders like torpedoes. A black man with a hat and glasses walked in with an icepick sticking out of his chest. When they dug the needle in me, I broke into a sweat and vomited.

At the bottom of Omega Street we turn right at Hamilton until we get to Larimer. Instead of turning at

Auburn for home, we keep going. I don't know what I'll do if we don't stop. The snow comes at us on a line as we lean into it, trudging up Larimer, cars with chains slowly clinking by, Christmas lights left on all night in the merchants' windows, the butcher's with a gutted pig hanging upside down, surrounded by green and red bulbs.

At Genevieve's we stop and Francene, still with my hand in hers, guides me in and we take a table. In an instant a waiter places a basket of warm Italian bread in front of us, and a saucer with butter pats. The restaurant is warm and not crowded, people at tables eating quietly, the lights low, a Christmas tree, colored lights and a silver garland strung around the bar, Italian Christmas records playing on the jukebox, all of it, even the music, reflected in bottles and glasses and the big mirror behind the bar.

Smoking at the bar, there's a big guy in a suit. His dark hair is combed back and stays—the way I wish my hair would look. What Francene calls "trained." With his glass of ice and blond water, he walks over to the table and sits with us. He and my mother kiss each other on the cheek. His name is Tardy and he knows me. He is close-shaved, but you can still see his black beard in points all over his face; and when he laughs his teeth are big and white as Chiclets.

We order a pizza. Tardy lights my mother's cigarettes with his big hands. He keeps asking her if he can buy her a drink. She laughs and tells him just Coke. I have chocolate milk and we talk about baseball. Tardy says he played ball for a while with Detroit, that he was friends with Hank Greenberg. Did I know Greenberg was Jewish? That Greenberg taught him to eat bagels and lox, and now every Saturday morning he eats bagels and lox for breakfast. He even went to temple with Greenberg and wore a yarmulke. Yiddish sounded to him like Latin. Even now, every once in a while, he'll go to a synagogue just to hear it. It changed the way he thought about Jews. And, Jesus, Greenberg could hit. He never got credit for how good he was because he was a Jew. Jews and Italians have a lot in common, really. They both like to eat. They both like kids. And neither of them like the *tizzones*. Tardy doesn't have kids, but he says he'll come and play ball with me some time. Maybe he'll take me to a Pirates game. Would I like that?

"Sure," I tell him and I half mean it. The half that likes sitting in the warm, glittering restaurant eating pizza with Francene and a strong, handsome guy with plenty of money who could be my father. I like the security of that other bookend. Like in the movie *Hondo*, when John Wayne takes up with Geraldine Page, whose husband is gone, and her son; and they pretend for a little while that they are a family, even though they can never be and the Apaches are lurking just beyond that illusion of safety.

But the other half is suspicious. About what he said about Greenberg and coming to play ball with me and the

Pirates game. He's pulling my leg. And I don't like the way he tilts his head to Francene's ear and whispers, how she laughs and looks at me to see if I am watching. When Francene leaves for the ladies room, Tardy pays our tab, and slips me two bucks.

Outside he and I throw snowballs at each other and then at Francene, standing at the corner of Larimer and Meadow catching snowflakes in her open mouth. They make starbursts on her red coat. She laughs. Cars stream down Larimer towards Saints Peter and Paul.

"Let's go to midnight Mass," she says.

We cruise down Larimer in Tardy's charcoal Imperial and park right in front of the church. He walks around and opens the door for Francene, then for me in the back seat. Francene takes my hand. Tardy, with his arm around her waist, guides her through the wrought-iron lintel, then up the stone stairs into the church. We all take holy water from the vestibule font and make the Sign of the Cross. My foot doesn't hurt at all.

In old rose vestments, Father Vita paces to the foot of the altar, kneels and drones: "*In Nomine Patris, et Filii, et Spiritus Sancti. Amen.*" On the gray stone walls between each of the fourteen stations are plain pine wreaths, and vases of holly and berries on the side altars of the Blessed Mother and Saint Joseph. I have never seen so many people in church, so much light and gladness. So unreal, like being in a movie. Not like we were being filmed, but that we *were* the movie being watched by real people somewhere as if we had become make-believe, the whole church and all the people inside it perfected inside one of those water-filled paperweights that swirl with snow when turned upside down. Wanting it to last forever, I simply sit there and let it wash over me, the entire church flickering with candlelight, incense and Latin carols like stuttering celluloid, frame by hypnotic frame, the surrounding stained glass carouseling until I am dizzy.

At the Consecration, just as Father Vita holds up the host and says, "*Hoc est enim Corpus meum*" (For this is My Body)—the point in the Mass that excites me most and of which I make sketch after sketch in school with colored pencils—Francene in a distant, panicky voice says, "I have to get out of here."

She clamps one of my hands and we jostle along the pew, stepping all over people until we get to the aisle, big Tardy following and just about knocking people over trying to squeeze through. Only three pews from the altar, Francene, towing me on my bad foot, half runs back down the long aisle, the entire congregation it seems escorting us with their eyes. Just before we crash through the giant doors, I see a cadre of nuns in the last pew, several of whom I know from school, stare quizzically at me and my family as I cover my face with my free hand.

For kicks, Tardy says, he fishtails each turn, laughing, though Francene does not laugh. She looks straight ahead at the snow disintegrating against the windshield. He asks me how I like it. I don't like it at all. It scares me. But I have learned that what you are scared of you never admit. You just ride it out and shut up and at least you have your dignity. You might even get over what you are afraid of. When Hondo found out the kid couldn't swim he threw him in the river and walked off. The kid learned to swim.

EAST LIBERTY

CHAPTER 5

When I wake up on Christmas morning, I don't remember anything more than feeling drowsy and lying down in the backseat of Tardy's car, then being carried by him into the house. I go to my window. The tree Francene and I had planned to put up and decorate the night before is still on the porch, on its side, matted with snow.

Smelling cigarette smoke and coffee, I pad into the kitchen where Francene sits with a cigarette in one hand and her other wrapped around a cup of coffee. She wears a red-piped silky robe with blue flamingos spread over it. Her hair is bunched in a scarf on top of her head. She looks like a girl. I stand in the doorjamb for a moment and witness her expression switch half a dozen times as if she is having an argument with herself.

When she notices me, her face lights up, "Hi, Bobby, honey, Merry Christmas," and she holds out her arms.

I walk into her arms and feel myself against her yielding, silky softness.

"We didn't put up the Christmas tree," I say.

"Honey, you fell asleep in the car."

"Who was that guy?"

"Just an old friend. Did you like him?"

"Why?"

"Oh, I don't know."

"Do you like him?"

Holding me tightly against her, she doesn't answer.

"I don't feel good," I say for no reason.

"What's the matter?"

"I don't know. My head hurts. My stomach."

"Sweetheart."

I bury my head into her neck and feel her warm skin against my face, smell her perfume. She scoops me into her lap and lays her palm against my forehead.

"You don't feel hot."

"I'm dizzy."

"Are you hungry?"

"I don't know."

"C'mon." She gets to her feet with me still in her lap and carries me—something she has not done for years, it seems—back into my room and puts me to bed.

"We never put up the tree," I say.

"Listen. That will be taken care of as soon as I bring you breakfast."

She props me up with extra pillows from her bed, then

serves me tea and toast and a soft-boiled egg. As I am eating she sets up the Christmas tree at the foot of my bed, and begins decorating it. She holds up each bulb and asks me where I want it placed on the tree. On my bedside table she sets up the chipped Nativity scene. Jesus's manger is Scotch-taped together and Mary's nose is gone. Two of the shepherds and all of the cattle are missing legs.

When the tree is decorated Francene plugs in the lights, then hauls the television set in from the living room, puts it on my dresser and crawls in bed and sits next to me.

"Do you feel any better, pigeon?"

"I don't know. Maybe."

"Did the food help?"

"I guess."

We live in my bedroom for the next few days, eating macaroni and cheese, cinnamon toast, canned biscuits, marshmallows toasted over the stove's gas burners, chocolate milk and bags of salted nuts and chocolate my mother gets free from work. My gift is a new Sears model fielder's glove with Don Blasingame's signature in the pocket and a cross web. It is blond and smells of musk. I have wanted it for so long, I can't believe it is mine. Because I can't get out of bed, Francene, using my old glove and the taped ball, catches with me across my room. From time to time she sprays herself with the perfume that is my Christmas gift to her, along with a tin of dusting powder that came with it.

We watch a lot of movies. *Miracle on 34th Street, It's a Wonderful Life, Holiday Inn, White Christmas, Heidi.* Lying there with Francene next to me, stealthily, like a soul transmigrating, I enter each film and live within its perfect boundaries, wandering the snow-blanketed big houses with their laid fires, and geometrically perfect pyramids of gifts beneath immense trees, gorging myself on their long candlelit tables and optimism. Even in her housecoat, Francene is the equal of Maureen O'Hara and Donna Reed. I marry her off to John Payne, James Stewart, Bing Crosby, and they produce for me a horde of rosy brothers and sisters.

As a family we sit around the piano and sing. We do nice things for the poor. My mother does housework wearing a dress and pearls and each evening my father arrives home from his office and sits through dinner in his habitual white shirt and necktie. My sweet and absentminded grandparents live next door. Above all there is plenty of money, and at every turn we profess our love for one another.

There is *A Christmas Carol*, too. A particularly old, scratched and spidery, gothic version, starring Alistair Sim, that could have been directed by Alfred Hitchcock. Despite the famous happy ending, and Scrooge's regeneration, it scares me with its apparitions and decidedly Catholic promise of hell. Nineteenth-century London has the same sooty edge as East Liberty. Too real, it is a film I don't wish to inhabit. The Cratchetts will see right through me. There are already enough ghosts orbiting my head. I feel like I should hurry to confession (I think with shame of having rushed out of midnight Mass) and beg for a happy ending since I still believe in them. I have not so much given up on Santa Claus, as he has given up on me.

I shouldn't have lied about being sick. It's like putting the eyes on yourself. *Stupido*. I manufacture just one Christmas vision of my father: It is a snowy Christmas Eve, darkness just settling. I ride with him to Stagno's for bread. He drives very carefully. We park right in front of the bakery.

"A loaf of crippled, please," my father says to Mrs. Tommarello who works the counter.

She smiles and repeats, "Loaf of crippled," then to me, "Cookie, honey?"

"Yes, please," I say and point to the cookie I always choose: a fluted vanilla sugar cookie with a fat, swirling cone of fudge on top. Carefully nibbling away all of the white part, I very slowly eat the fudge.

As my father backs out of his space, he skids and nudges a car that has just parked behind us. There is the sound of broken glass. We get out and see that a headlight is smashed and the fender dented. The driver, with a boy about my age, surveys the damage. He wears a blue coat and jacket with orange patches that say GULF on them. His hands are black with grease and he needs a shave.

"Jeez, I'm sorry," says my father. "I hit a little patch of ice."

The other guy has his hands together at his waist, and he opens them up, like *These things happen.* It's freezing cold. "Hey, no one was hurt," he says, and puts his hand on his boy's head. The kid holds on to his dad.

My father yanks out his wallet and thumbs through his cards. "I have insurance. We'll be glad to take care of everything. Let me give you my name and phone number."

"I appreciate that, buddy. But would you mind if I just run in and get a loaf of bread before they close?"

"No. No. Go ahead."

My father and I get back in our car which is still running. He turns the heater all the way up, lights a cigarette and sings, "Cigarettes and whiskey and wild, wild women. They'll do you no harm, but they'll bring you to shame." We watch through Stagno's big front window the man and his son. The boy points to the cookie he wants and Mrs. Tommarello, smiling, hands it to him. The boy offers the man the cookie. He takes a bite and smiles.

At this juncture, my vision goes sour. Even that won't come out right. My father climbs out of the car, scoops up a handful of exhaust-blackened snow and coats our license plate with it. He jumps in the car and we take off. The man, holding his bread, sees this, runs out the door with his son and chases us in his car. To escape, my father drives like a madman, but the man stays with us. I watch him through our rear window, one arm on the wheel and the other like a bar holding his son against his seat.

At the hairpin where the Spignos Club sits at the confluence of Hoeveler, Hamilton and Omega, we spin out 360, but my father stays with it, making a sudden right at Prince and gunning it down Negley Run for the Hollow.

It is here that the other man gives up, his one-eyed car fishtailing in slow motion gently into the curb. His boy seems to catch my eye as we both disappear into the darkness and all I can see is the bat, like a fake bat, flapping on the linoleum in its death throes, my father, in his white shirt, standing above it, wiping the sleep from his eyes as if he can't believe that anything is real.

• • •

The telephone rings and rings, but Francene will not answer it.

"Why don't you answer it?" I ask.

"I don't know. Let it ring."

Five, six times a day, but Francene refuses to pick it up, and forbids me to. It could be my father on the phone, but she will not answer it. I lie in my bed, feeling weaker and weaker from the curse I have turned on myself. The phone rings and rings and rings. I call for Francene to answer it, but I cannot unfasten my mouth. Then I remember. The rusty nail. I must have lockjaw.

Like my grandfather, my mouth has rusted shut and I

will never speak again. Like Ebenezer Scrooge I will live inside my own bitterness until I am invaded by shades. Someone knocks insistently at our door. Open the door, the knuckles insist. My father come to rescue us. But Francene refuses to budge. She hasn't dressed in days. She lights another cigarette and reads the thermometer.

"Jesus," she says, then peels out of her robe and rips the rag out of her hair, lifts off her nightgown and runs around the room getting dressed. I hear her in the kitchen calling a cab.

"I'm going to go after Nonna," she says. "I'll be back very soon. I promise. Will you be okay?"

"Yes." But I'm not so sure.

While we wait for the cab, she gets me out of my wet pajamas and into dry ones.

"I'll turn on the TV, pigeon," she says, kisses me, then she's gone.

The movie is *Premature Burial* with Ray Milland, about a cataleptic so obsessed with being buried alive that he constructs an elaborate plan to escape the tomb. It is not the kind of movie I would ever watch alone, but I can't summon the strength to get up and turn it off. I apparently doze off because when I wake, Francene still not home, the darkness cushioning the man in his coffin is the same color as the growing dusk on the other side of the window, and I am scared, but not sure if I am dreaming, not sure if Ray

Milland is dreaming as he triggers the springlock inside the coffin and steps out of it into the burial vault. He takes the lid off a chalice to drink of the water he has laid by and it foams with worms. I think I scream, but it is the phone ringing, and I run dizzily into the kitchen and pick it up.

"Bobby," says the voice.

"Uh huh."

"This is dad. You remember me? I'm on my way over to drop off your Christmas presents."

On the kitchen table is my mother's drained dirty glass lined with buttermilk scurf, a shotglass, two empty bottles of Iron City, a shelled half grapefruit pocked with snuffed out Kents and Camels, a tube of lipstick, mascara. A necktie dangles from a chairback. I sink into the chair and stare at the blackness pushing like hands against the kitchen window, the pane expanding in and out like a balloon until the darkness enters and seats itself across from me and smiles.

If I pretend it is not there, if I do not look at it and refuse to answer if it speaks, it will go away. It drums its fingers on the table. I gaze above its head at the Madonna on the wall above the sink. I say one Hail Mary after another.

"Bobby," says the darkness.

"Holy Mary, Mother of God," I say to myself, because my jaws are sealed shut, hoping the Blessed Mother will hop off the wall and speak as she does so often in movies.

"It's all your fault, Bobby. Every bit of it. And you know it."

"Pray for us sinners." The entire house is dark, but I can't move to switch on a light.

"Everything is a lie. Nothing works."

"Now and at the hour of our death. Amen."

There is someone at the door. Jacob Marley in his cerements of chain. No. My father. He said he'd come. I rise to answer the door.

"Stay seated," the darkness commands, turning toward the door as the jamb gives and the rusty hinges screak.

"Honey, it was just a dream," Francene is saying, holding me to her. "Look, I brought Nonna back to get you well. It was just a dream. It's okay."

Nonna stands behind Francene, the black rag of her head dotted with snow. Her gold teeth stand out in a smile. Just a dream, she tells me. *Sogno.* She sits next to Francene on the bed and presses her lips to my forehead. Garlic. The lips fretting parsley as they gauge my temperature, kissing me as they lift and say, "*Benedire*, Roberto."

What I know I know through smell—medicinal rubber, rubbing alcohol and carbolated Vaseline; and sound—the bathroom closet rifled, running water, scrubbing, the antiseptic hush of the women whispering behind the door.

"Run," warns the darkness, establishing itself in the chair at my bedside.

Carrying the red and black enema hoses and bladders, Francene and Nonna appear like witch doctors out of a Tarzan movie and hold me facedown on towels against my bed until I am brimming with hot, soapy water.

Then I do run. Into the bathroom to sit, naked for my pajama shirt, on the cracked wooden seat, my insides streaming out of me like the dancing gas flames in the little white heater beside the toilet.

Nonna sleeps in Francene's bed and Francene on a pallet in my room. I hear the darkness leave his perch at my bed and go to her. I hear her murmur in her sleep. Nonna prowls the house all night with a flashlight, checking my temperature with her parsley and garlic mouth. The darkness cannot abide the room when she is in it. Nonno sits in the chair where darkness had been. There is a voice inside him, but he has no mouth, only the eel mustaches.

I stand at the stove, my yellow slicker tenting my head, and breathe in the eucalyptus boiling in the giant sauce pot. For the *catarro*. And lemon, honey, and elderberry brandy. Garlic soup.

Nonno marches into the kitchen and slams down a tin of hot mustard seed and linseed oil. He and Nonna make a yellow, unctious paste of it, spread it on a white towel and glue it to my chest. I lie in bed under the covers, the mustard plaster burning me all the way to my backbone until I have no chest, just a cauterized cavity where my heart had been.

Nonno sits next to me in darkness's place, refraining from the diNobilis, sipping anisette and coffee, trying to reteach himself to talk.

One afternoon Nonna walks in with a bowl and sits in darkness's chair. She feeds me, spoon by spoon, the most delicious soup I have ever eaten. The fever parchment coating my lips dissolves and I swallow it with the broth.

"What is it Nonna?" I ask. "What makes it so good?"

She almost giggles. "I can't tell," she says and holds an index finger to her lips. *Segreto.*

Francene traipses in. She has taken to dressing again, and has returned to work. "So you can talk," she says.

There is a morning I wake, and Nonna is disappeared. I smell her in each room as I wander the house. It is cleaner than I have ever seen it, the refrigerator filled with things we never buy. The darkness has left East Liberty, in its place the sun off the snow shining through each of our dazzling windows. At the mirror, I see that there is something different about me. I am darker, my brows heavier and on my lip a few barely noticeable hairs. Behind me Francene suddenly appears, her hair prismatic from the sun beaming through the window and off the mirror. She puts her hands on my shoulders and we look at each other through the mirror. My head rests just under her chin.

On New Year's Eve we drink eggnog, eat fishsticks and french fries and watch Guy Lombardo at Times Square.

Along with him, Francene sings "Auld Lang Syne" and
promises that some day she'll take me there to watch the
ball drop, something she's always wanted to do. We count
"5-4-3-2" and at midnight kiss and clink our glasses together,
switch the channels and watch A Streetcar Named Desire.

I see a little bit of Francene, mainly the tender parts, in
Blanche, but I don't much like Vivien Leigh as a blonde.
There is at once a hardness and fragility to her, and maybe
I realize for the first time that you can be two people at
once, maybe even more. It makes me want to protect
Francene. We never talk about the movies we watch.
Nineteen sixty-one is a little more than two hours old. The
year West Side Story is released, which changes East Liberty,
long in love with gangsters, forever.

Everyone rushes out to see the movie, even Francene,
who goes with Poe's mother. On every turntable in the
neighborhood, ours included, the soundtrack plays nonstop.
The album comes with a little booklet that synopsizes the
movie, so I know the whole story of love and gang warfare
and can sing each song along with the record.

Nearly overnight, a band of hoods, led by a big-bellied,
curly-haired teenager named Dominic Fusca, forms and dubs
themselves the Jets after the white gang in the movie. There
isn't a wall in East Liberty that isn't spray-painted with JETS
and FUCK.

Chain-smoking, Dom and his boys roam in white T-shirts, tight, iridescent stovepipes and pointy, cleated, black shoes that tie on the sides. With their girlfriends, who wear halters and peroxide their black hair, and are fighters too, the Jets commandeer the Hollow, and take up residence with their girls in the abandoned treehouses. They carry BB pistols, killing rabbits and squirrels and cooking them over fires down in the woods, and hack into one another with switchblades homemade cursive tattoos that read JETS. It is said, too, that they take "dope," whatever that means. The few times I cross their paths with Francene, they whistle at her; and once, as she, holding tightly to my hand, walked silently by, ignoring the gang, Dom himself grabbed one of his confederate's T-shirts and ripped it right off him. Occasionally you see SHARKS sprayed on a building, but I never see them, the purported rival black gang that lives in the projects on an escarpment across the Hollow. I make it my business to stay clear of the Jets.

●　●　●

One evening, just after Francene gets off work, there is a phone call. Nonno has had a stroke. We don't have a car, and Francene does not want to wait for a streetcar. She clamps me by a hand and tows me down Lincoln to Nonna's house, which seems like miles away. It is winter dusk and the sky darkening. The streetlights are on, headlights from the traffic boring into us. She hurts my hand, whispering over and over, "Oh, my God," trying, I'm sure, not to cry, as her long red coat beats about her in the freezing wind.

When we get to my grandparents', word has just come from the hospital that Nonno is dead, and it is then that I see my mother cry for the first and only time in my life. She sits there on Nonna's couch, next to a lamp with reliefs of naked angels on it, and sobs. Still in her red coat and wearing a white sweater and big domed pearl earrings that screw onto her ears, she holds a handkerchief to her mouth and whimpers like a dog in pain, but trying not to give in, as the tears pour out of her spooky, verdigris eyes.

There are plenty of other people there, none of whom I know, crying too, but my mother sits alone, smelling of salt and chocolate and smoke. I smell her from across the room. I don't feel like crying at all. I am merely hungry. When Nonna arrives from the hospital, her eyes first settle on Francene with what I recognize as reproach. Then she collapses on the couch next to her and they hold each other's hands and cry. I don't really know the difference between grief and anger, so I walk into the kitchen where the table is spread with food, and people are eating, and help myself. Before we leave to go back home, Nonna gives Francene some money.

EAST LIBERTY

Chapter 6

Every morning I wake to my alarm and the empty house. In the kitchen the radio plays: a tractor-trailer overturned in Blawnox, traffic stalled inbound on the Liberty Bridge, the windchill at fifteen. My cup of hot chocolate, cold by the time I get to it, sits on the table next to my lunch, milk money, and doorkey. I skim the curdled skin off it and drink it and my juice while I eat my cereal. Then I bundle up, strap on my bookbag and black buckle-arctics, check the door several times to make sure I locked it, and trudge alone to school between two walls of plowed snow. Down Lincoln to Mayflower, a left at Paulson, a right at Auburn, then another left onto Larimer Avenue where the entire block between Hamilton and Booze Alley is bastioned by Saints Peter and Paul Church; the rectory; the convent; Divine Providence Academy, an all-girls high school; and the eight-room red-brick grade school, blessed on the first Sunday in September of 1906, where I spend dreamy and undercover days under the tutelage of the Sisters of Divine Providence.

I like very much the astringent severity and order of their parochial world, so unlike the hurdy-gurdy one I live in with Francene. Each day commences with eight o'clock Mass of the Catechumens. I perch in the choir loft, shelved high in the back of the church, with the rest of the choir, singing in Latin and staring at Pat, the organist and choir director. She is a young, blonde woman who wears glasses and soft sweaters. Unlike the nuns, her teeth are white and perfect, and her mouth is always circled wetly around one of those round Latin vowels as we sing the *Sanctus* and *Agnus Dei*, the organ revving like a fighter engine and the echo of Father Vita's lilting recitation beating about us. A storey below, all eight grades and their sisters, as well as the shut-ins from the convent, and scattered parishioners, deploy among the yew and marble and stained glass. But it is also at Saints Peter and Paul that I realize the dilemma of my fatherless state. I've always felt that people know things about me that I don't know myself, but nowhere is this sense more acute than at school among the nuns. They look at me as if I am damaged, the way they look at those frail iconographic illustrations in our religion book of brown and yellow and red pagan children desperate for Catholic conversion before being ripped apart by jackals.

My impression is that they cease talking when I walk into a room and tsk-tsk at my appearance. There is something obviously tragic about me. On the nights of open house, the sisters send me with my reader to the cloakroom; then they walk to the front of the room, under the big walled crucifix, and confer in whispers with Francene. I steal glimpses through the door. Francene, looking so very young, like a child herself, smiles embarrassedly the entire time and nods her head at everything they say. Frequently they give her rosaries and holy cards which she sticks in the edges of her bedroom mirror. But sometimes she throws them down in the street when we leave the schoolhouse and tows me home by the hand without talking, but mumbling "those witches." If I ask her, she simply says, "It's nothing. It's not you. You're a good boy. People just don't know how to mind their business."

I have no problems at school. In fact the case could be made that I am the smartest boy in the room. My teachers bring in the principal, Sister Gertrude, and Father Vita, the pastor, just to hear me read. But they too seem privy to secret knowledge and possess the habits of eyeing me piously with their heads to one shoulder. Little by little, as I am promoted to the next grade and then the next, they begin talking to me about a vocation, the way other kinds of boys are talked to about the armed services.

I begin drawing, almost pathologically, pictures of the priest, his back to the congregation at Consecration. I am not much of an artist, so I choose this pose because I don't have to draw the priest's face. Just his brightly vestured broad back, two gold slashes for the cross emblazoned on it, and a black stump for his head. No appendages holding aloft the host or the chalice, either, because I can't draw hands. The same sorry picture over and over. But it seems to excite the nuns, as if it underscores my subconscious declaration for a vocation. It is as if, to them, priesthood is my only barter to salvage my tainted blood. It is obvious that other kids draw better; but they have fathers. At least that's the way I reckon it.

Micky D'Andrea, a truly gifted artist, draws priests all the time too. Perfect in every way. Hands, faces, every detail photographic. He can draw Christ on the Cross, flanked by the two thieves, down to the sweat beads on the doomed Savior's forehead. But he is what the nuns call "willful" and lacking in self-control, and they beat him all the time. Which, even though I have nothing against him, pleases me because I resent him for his perfect drawing.

Sister bends Mickey over her desk and pounds him with a board. Over and over, his hair poofing up with the gust and impact of every strike. After each beating he peels himself off the desk, turns and says, "Thank you, Sister," as is the custom.

"You are welcome, Mr. D'Andrea," Sister replies.

Then he looks at me and smiles. I overhear Francene say that his father, a bartender at Nardini's, writes numbers on the side. Which isn't much of a father, she says.

In the sixth grade, one day at recess, Mickey slips me a

sketch of a naked woman, so carnally rendered, the crotch especially, that I nearly faint. God help me, I keep that drawing in my clutched and sweaty fingers for days and days, slipping it out to gape at it until it literally falls apart. But by that time I don't need it any more. The image of that woman has made my mind its disorderly house, and there is nothing I can do to evict her.

The next morning I march into school and inform Sister that Mickey has shown me a dirty picture of a woman he had drawn. Sister Gertrude is summoned, and Mickey is beaten with a Calvinist fury I have never before witnessed. Each time I think she is finished, the board descends again, Mickey's Buster Brown hair luffing up and going dead. When he staggers away from the desk he's been crooked over, it is obvious he is hurt badly. But he thanks Sister, looks straight at me, and smiles.

That afternoon he follows me home, remaining half a block behind me, stopping every time I stop to look back at him. I am not afraid he will jump me. I can beat his brains out in my sleep. He is a spindly, almost sickly, kid with dark circles under his eyes and yellowish skin and eyes. It isn't that. It is my own shame that I have told on him, and how he has been beaten as a result. It makes me want to kill him, I am so ashamed.

"You better get out of here," I yell at him.

"Why'd you tell on me?"

"You better get out of here."

"I thought we were friends. Why'd you tell on me?"

I stand there watching him as he walks toward me. When he gets to within the length of my arm I am going to punch him. He isn't my damned conscience. But when he gets that close, I see that he is crying, and I can't do anything but stare at him. He looks like a refugee.

"Why'd you tell on me, Bobby?"

"I don't know. I'm sorry."

I don't know what else to say. Here is this kid who laughed—after having had the living hell kicked out of him by a nun—crying because he feels betrayed. I really don't know why I told. I despise stool pigeons. I want to die. We are standing on Paulson Avenue in front of Victoria Beverage, a beer distributor. For some reason they are closed, but there are stacks of wooden cases with empties in them next to the cellar door.

"You're sorry?" Mickey asks.

"Yes, I am. I don't know why I did it."

"If you're really sorry, then take one of those beer bottles and throw it out in the street in front of the next car that comes by."

"You're crazy."

"If you're sorry, do it."

I grab a brown, long bottle out of a case. A green-and-white Chevy rolls slowly down the street, and as it passes by, I whip the bottle. It explodes just in front of the front tires, which crunch over the shattered glass before the car halts. Mickey and I take off, but not before I see the driver, an old black lady, wearing a hat, put her hand to her chest and rock back in her seat. We run for a long time, but before we split up, he hands me a slippery piece of paper that has been folded several times into a small square.

I know what it is just by the feel of it, and Mickey's look of reproach when he put it in my hand, but I wait until I reach home to unfold it. Another picture of a naked woman. This time it is not a drawing, but a glossy, color photograph torn out of a magazine. A blonde woman wearing only a black velvet tassel around her neck and splayed out on a fainting couch. It is tracked with fingerprints and cigarette burns. The creases have worn the colors away so that a white grid crisscrosses it. The woman herself seems bored, having been looked at for so long by so many that she really doesn't care anymore. Still I find her beautiful in a terrible way, like photographs of dead people you occasionally see in magazines. It is beyond my power to look away, and finally, after days of staring at it, I take a match to it, throw it in the toilet, and flush.

Sometimes after school Mickey takes me up to Nardini's where his dad tends bar. It is on the corner of Hoeveler and Collins and has glass brick windows with neon Duquesne and Stoney's beer signs hanging in them.

An old, fat, blind guy named Mooch constantly sits outside the bar, no matter the weather, on a rattan chair. He wears a green tam o'shanter and plaid suit. Lying under his chair is a wizened, little, yellow dog that looks like a beagle without the spots. I've never seen it move. It is blind, too. Set up next to Mooch is an upended wooden crate on which he keeps his alms cup, a pint of Four Roses sheathed in a brown paper bag, and a jar of lubeans from which he habitually eats, chewing them up in his wide toothless mouth that collapses like a watery squinting eye, and then spitting the skins out on the sidewalk.

He gets his cup filled by telling fortunes and predicting the future. He knows people by their footfalls and smells. Not a person passes without his calling out a name or some prognostication like "Patterson'll go down in the fourth round," "Snow by midnight," "Play the number of your firstborn's birth date," "Don't marry that son of a bitch."

Usually people throw coins in the cup and keep walking, but quite a few stop and ask his advice on things. I figure him for just another East Liberty sideshow, but Mickey, to whom he always confides with great gravity, "You're going to be a great artist," believes in him. To me he always says, "You're Francesca Renzo's boy." While this does not amount to much in the way of sooth, I find it eerie that he knows this, and I always manage a nickel or dime to throw in the cup. Anything, really, to not have to look at him.

Nardini's is dark, smoke hovering about the long pool table lights, the bar lined mainly with mute old guys who sport battered, old hats and nurse shots and beers all day. Mickey's dad doesn't really look like a bartender. Day in and day out in an open-collared white shirt and black suit pants, he has a pasty bookishness. He oils his blond hair straight back so that it seems darker, and on top where you can see scalp streaking through it, it sits stiff like a duck's ruff. Outside of the nuns, he is the only person I have ever seen who wears wire spectacles. He treats me really well, but Mickey is afraid of him, and he says his mother is too.

During the war, Mickey's dad was a paratrooper. Now he walks with a limp, and I never see him without a glass of VO and water in his hand. He owns a German Luger he took off a dead Nazi in Paris. Mickey says Mr. D'Andrea isn't his real dad, but I don't know what he means.

I like hanging around Nardini's. It beats going home to the empty house, and it's getting so I don't like playing ball with only a brick wall for company anymore. Mickey's dad sets us up at a pool table and gives us pickled eggs, Slim Jims, and Dad's root beer.

In the back room, a poker game is going, but the door opens only when Mickey's dad delivers a tray of drinks or one of the guys comes out to use the bathroom. A pay phone on the wall rings every few minutes for Mickey's dad. He pulls out the pad and pencil he keeps in his shirt pocket and writes something down. Mickey and I usually stay an hour or so, long enough to play a game or two of pool and have a snack. I have to make sure I'm home before Francene gets there.

Other days, we wander all over East Liberty, past the Cameraphone and its bill of dirty movies with names like *Nudes of All Nations* and *Nudes in the Sun*, the posters outside scorched with images of half-clad women, furtive silhouettes of men slumped in the darkened lobby.

We stop in Mansmann's long enough to steal something meaningless. A key fob or a shoehorn. Often we lift penny candy from Kresge's and Woolworth's. If we come upon a condemned building, we blast the glass out of it with rocks. Mickey takes awful chances, walking across bridge ledges and shinnying up drainpipes, hanging from roofs by his toes and climbing over two-storey cyclone fences topped with barbed wire. Sometimes I can't stand to be with him; he makes me so nervous. In broad daylight, he breaks streetlights and pushes over paper boxes.

At Mass, each morning, singing the Kyrie in the choirloft, I resolve to give up my life with Mickey. My soul is crawling with sin; I must confess. I still draw priests all the time and, though I still ponder becoming one, and play along with the sisters when they quiz me about a vocation, I know I'll never follow through. Besides, *Boystown* is bullshit. There aren't any Father Flanagans. No Spencer

Tracys. No Bing Crosbys, Gene Kellys or Pat O'Briens. There is Father Vita who bawls you out during confession and talks about money, not Jesus, during his homilies. Francene says she smells Scotch on his breath and I have heard my grandmother say his housekeeper is his *commare*.

Nevertheless, I love the nuns. They load me up with scapulars and medals and prayerbooks for winning spelling bees and being the best reader. After school, sometimes I stay and wash the boards and clean erasers. As a reward, they take me to the convent kitchen and pet me and feed me cake and prattle on about my eventual priesthood. I look around that sterilized, sinless world, literally vibrating with sanctifying grace, and think, "Yes, yes, yes."

But by the end of the day I am with Mickey again, and he slips me a picture or takes me to the bar, and then we steal and break things on the way home.

Mickey's pictures continue to get better, so real they look like photographs. But on his drawings of priests, saints and angels, and even Jesus, he has begun to include nearly imperceptible flaws. An eye is askew, or they are missing a finger or a toe. Little things. A smirk or a leer. An earring. Whenever the nuns notice, they punish him. I no longer can stand to see him beaten.

Each time the wood falls on him it is like my teeth are clicking and the center of me detonating. Mickey still smiles through the whole thing, his darkish, yellow face screwed up with pain, his eyes on me until I drop mine with shame at the thought of the time I made him cry, not by beating him, but by betraying him. I don't want any more of it, but I can't stay away from him. In my pockets are rosaries and dirty pictures.

When we get to Nardini's that day, Mooch says to Mickey, "You're going to fall."

"And you're going to grow eyeballs," Mickey cracks.

Transparent lubean skins dot the prone blind dog.

"Francesca Renzo's son, the priest," Mooch croaks at me. He eats a bowl of tripe from the bar. It drips from his rubber mouth and chin.

Mickey and I play pool for a while, then go into the bathroom. We have a few metal slugs, so we try substituting them for change in the rubber machine, but they jam up the coin slot. The woman on the machine wears a G-string and nothing on top. Her hands cup her breasts. A dead ringer for Ida Lupino, she leans over and looks at us. When we can't get the knob to turn, Mickey beats on it.

Suddenly his father busts through the door.

"What's all that pounding? The walls are shaking out there. What the hell are you two doing in here?"

Then he spies the slug in the coin slot. He tries the knob, and when he sees it's stuck, he bashes Mickey across the head, then again and again, throwing him off the plywood walls like a rag and slamming him in the head every time he bounces back. Mickey doesn't laugh or cry; he just crosses his arms over his head and face and slides down to the cement floor. But his dad still doesn't let up.

I tear out of there and don't stop running until I hit Mayflower Street. I can't believe how Mickey's dad beat him. Even after he was on the floor. I'm scared, and wish Francene would be home when I get there. Suddenly I'm conscious of someone coming up behind me, and turn. Two black kids. I pick up my pace a little. Turning again, I see they are a little closer. When I cross the street, and they follow, I definitely know something is up and break into a jog. Hearing their tennis shoes flapping on the pavement, I get scared and start to sprint, but I am already played out with running from Nardini's.

I cross Paulson without even looking. The two behind me get held up by traffic; but suddenly black kids, boys and girls, seem to appear out of nowhere and I am surrounded. Lowering my head, I bowl through a couple of them, but they swarm me, and no matter how hard I fight I can't break away. I'm dragged a half block up to Lincoln School, then into one of the abandoned side schoolyards facing Frankstown Avenue. Several of them are much older than I am, but some my age too. They tell me to take my clothes off. I tell them I won't, and a big girl, who seems to be in charge, slaps me. I attempt to run, but she slaps me again, grabs my coat and starts pulling it off.

I scream, but my voice drowns in car horns and the screech of trolley brakes along Frankstown. My coat is ripped off and then my shirt. They are undoing my belt and yanking off my T-shirt when an old black guy, with white hair, white beard, and dressed all in white like a painter, comes charging across the schoolyard with a tire iron.

"Get out of here," he yells and waves the tire iron.

The little kids scatter, but the bigger ones square off until the old man takes a few swipes at them and then they back off too and start walking away.

"Go on about your business, you devils," he hollers after them.

I am on the ground, curled up.

"C'mon, little fella," he says, helping me up. "Nobody gonna hurt you."

I buckle my belt. He helps me get my coat on. The zipper is stripped and a sleeve hangs. We don't even bother with the shirt. He smells of turpentine and liquor and his eyes are white, his skin so dark it shines in the sun like a waxed black car.

Throwing down the tire iron, he takes me by the hand and walks me down the street to my house where we sit on the porch watching traffic. We don't speak, but I leave my hand in his until Francene arrives from work. He motions her aside for a moment and they talk; then he walks off our porch and disappears.

Within a week we move to a second-floor apartment in a triplex on Collins Avenue, right across the street from Mickey's house, a half block from Nardini's. Stagno's is just around the corner, and from my bedroom window I can look out over the Hollow. School and church are just a ten-minute walk. But the best part about the move to Collins Avenue is that it's crawling with kids. Finally blessed with living people to play ball with, I spend every day that the weather permits at Dilworth Schoolyard or Peabody Field.

I still spend plenty of time at the bar with Mickey. The beating his dad gave him never comes up, but he tells me once he'll someday kill him.

"You know, I wouldn't mind not having an old man," he always says.

We have taken to stealing a few bottles of beer from the bar and smuggling them down the Hollow where we crouch in the woods and sip them, eat crabapples, puff off Mickey's cigarettes and look at seedy pictures he draws or has stolen.

"It's all about art," Mickey says.

We spy on people in the bushes, splayed out, grunting on top of each other, or throw rocks at bands of roving black kids from the projects and then run from them. We smash our empty bottles in the boulevard.

What's happening to me? I don't like the taste of beer or cigarettes, and every time I look at one of the pictures my head swims and I get sick to my stomach. One day after Mickey and I separate after leaving the Hollow, I watch two high school kids pressed together between two of the houses in the alley behind our house. He has his hand underneath her shirt, and they kiss beyond what I've seen in any movie. There is at once a tremendous beauty and horror about it that invades me like a drug. I get so dizzy I pass out. When I wake up in the weeds, I know that I need Confession.

• • •

By the time I'm in seventh grade, I'm so good at nine ball that some of the guys from the poker game come out from the back and run racks with me. Mickey's no competition. When we're at the bar, he spends more and more of his time drawing: the high vinyl-topped stools, a hatrack, salt-and-pepper shakers, the cigarette machine he renders so realistically that if you pulled one of the knobs a pack of Luckies would fall out. I rationalize that pool, like baseball, is a game. There is nothing wrong with it. Sometimes they invite me into the back and I sit and watch and listen as they play poker, a pile of green bills circled in smoke on the green felt-topped card table. I like the rhythm of poker, the quiet nervy ride around the table until only one guy's left, like the bottom of the ninth. Mickey's dad pays us a little change to deliver drinks and sandwiches to them. They're good guys and sometimes they press a few bucks on me. Some of them say they know Francene and ask how she's doing. I just say, "Okay." She has strictly forbidden me to be anywhere near Nardini's.

From outside I hear Mooch call, "Francesca Renzo," and at first it doesn't register. I think he's talking to me, so I walk out of the back room and there is Francene, standing with her hands on her hips in the bar, when she should be behind the candy counter at Sears, the late afternoon sun slanting in through the window.

I am speechless, but not just because Francene has just caught me red-handed and I am in a peck of trouble. It's the way she stands there in the light with her hands on her hips and that big red coat of hers flowing behind her and the feather in her hat like a lightning bolt, her long hair filled with sparks. She is a cross between the Blessed Mother and Merle Oberon, so beautiful I am worried she'll break into flames. The guys come out from the back and just stand there. Mickey's dad is frozen behind the bar. Mickey collapses in a chair.

"Let's go," she says.

I walk over to her. She seizes my hand and we walk out of the bar.

Mooch says, "Francesca Renzo and her boy priest." And then he laughs, which is when I realize I'm in trouble.

EAST LIBERTY

CHAPTER 7

No one ever calls Mickey Mickey again after he falls off the Hoeveler Street Bridge. He forfeits that name forever and becomes Platehead because, among other things, they put a plate in his head. This is a puzzling concept to me. I guess I should ask someone, but for a long time I conceive of it as a china dinner plate in his head, and wonder why in the world they'd stick a dish in someone's head. Even after Francene explains that it is a metal plate inserted to stabilize his smashed skull and protect his brain, I still see it sitting just on the other side of his forehead with a napkin and cutlery on either side of it. Anyhow his head doesn't look any different for having a plate in it, but the rest of him surely does. It's like when you kill a spider, how it instantly shrivels before your eyes. His limbs are no good at all.

Even in the hottest weather, a blanket drapes his legs, his feet with black hightops twisted at oblique angles visible below the hem. His chest is sunken, his hands drawn into claws and strapped to the wheelchair arms. Only in the very coldest weather is he not out on the porch in the wheelchair, watching the traffic whiz along Collins Avenue. He can only stare straight ahead, his head clamped by a headrest like in a dentist's chair, his tongue lolling out.

Sister takes the whole seventh grade to see him in the hospital, but he closes his eyes when we walk in and doesn't open them until we leave, tears seeping out and rolling down his yellow cheeks. His tongue, stitched because he had bitten it in the fall, hangs out of his mouth, black catgut in the shape of a pitchfork.

When he first comes home from the hospital, I spend a lot of time, at Francene's insistence, just sitting next to him on his porch. But there's little to say, and I feel bad being around him. He can talk, but he almost never does. All we really have in common are dirty pictures, vandalism, and theft. Plus, in his silence, it's like he's peering into my black heart. Like he took the fall for me. Like a sacrificial lamb.

It gets so I can't stand being around him, and little by little I stop visiting him. I yell to him and wave, but I don't hang with him on his porch, and neither does anyone else. Even though he stops going to school, I can't get away from him. Our kitchen window looks down on his porch where day after day he sits, bundled and hunched in his wheelchair like a gargoyle haunting Collins Avenue. When I walk out our front door, there he is. You can't miss him; he is like a fifteenth Station of the Cross. Platehead. Another player in East Liberty's cast of misfits. How it loves deformity. Like Mooch or Montmorrissey Hilliard, or any of the neighborhood freaks that parents point out to their children as warnings. Parables in the flesh.

I'm unable to look at him without thinking of how I ratted on him, Sister bashing him with that board, his hair floating up and that sickly sallow smile. The real tragedy, of course, is that he'll never draw anymore. The last time Mickey opened his mouth to me, the last time I saw that defiant, pitiful grin of his—even in the wheelchair—he said, like he knew that everything was bullshit, "It's all about art, Bobby." I don't know what he was talking about. Sometimes I feel as if I pushed him off the bridge.

With no one to beat, the nuns seem a little sad without Mickey. They shape his fall into allegory: the shocking true story of what happens to devilish boys. There is talk that it wasn't a fall, that he jumped, that he was drunk, that it was a Jets' gang initiation. What everyone seems to agree on is that he got what was coming to him, and the real sufferers are his parents.

While I despise them for using him this way, I don't totally disagree. If you're bad, bad things happen to you. Even God likes to get even, and that's why he threw Mickey off the bridge. But I don't know who he was getting even with—me or Mickey. Every time I see him drooling in that chair, framed in our kitchen window, I add another brick of guilt to the hod across my shoulders. If he wasn't crippled, if I didn't have to see him first and last every day when I check the weather, I wouldn't have to feel so bad about the things we've done together. About how I betrayed him to the nuns and how they beat him.

I stop drawing priests. I never could draw anyhow and I know it. The least I can do for Mickey, the real artist who can no longer use his hands, is quit pretending to be an artist myself. I decide to denounce my pipe dream about the priesthood, even though I figure it might be the only thing to save me. I'll play ball. Period. I don't really care about anything.

• • •

A few months after Mickey's accident, detouring on the way home from school through all Mickey's and my old haunts in the main shopping district of East Liberty, I walk into the National Record Mart on Penn Avenue. I have nothing in mind whatsoever. The spring sun drills through the huge storefront windows and sparkles off the tiered racks of black singles. It is hard for me to think about Mickey without seeing him bent over Sister's desk or taking his dad's backhands in the bar.

As a little kid, Mickey had a Cape Canaveral set, plastic rockets and planes and hangars. He'd spread it out on the living room floor and play with it all day. One day his mother and father got into a fight in the kitchen. Screaming and things hurled against the walls. Mickey crawled into a corner behind a chair and covered his ears. His father, still swearing at his mother, bulled through the room; and when he saw the Cape Canaveral set in the middle of the carpet, he kicked it over and crunched it to pieces under his shoes.

I decide that maybe Mickey might like a record to cheer him up. A little present. The only one on duty is an older black guy, beige, really, with a process and a long, skinny mustache like someone had dragged eyeliner just over the bow of his upper lip. He wears ribbed socks—we call them pimp socks—through which his skin shines. There are three other shoppers in the store, one of whom talks to the black clerk up at the front counter. A cut from *West Side Story*, "A Boy Like That," plays on the store turntable: "A boy who kills cannot love, a boy who kills has no heart."

I stroll up and down the racks until I come to "Kisses Sweeter Than Wine," a song I really like. There is the sound of a tinkling bell as the front door swings open. I turn my head to it and see the clerk and everyone else in the store turn also to the sound of the bell as another customer walks in.

Out on Penn Avenue the cars seem to still and the sound of the white-gloved traffic cop's whistle swells and then holds its pitch in my throat while the sun flashes, momentarily blinding me like a monstrous camera. I lift my sweatshirt and stuff the record down the front of my pants. Then everything begins to beat again. I hear the music and watch the cars rumble over the car tracks and the cop choreographing traffic. The clerk turns back to his conversation. For another ten minutes I browse the store, very deliberately picking up and studying 45s, then returning them to the rack.

On my way out, the clerk steps out from the counter and stands smiling in front of the door. He smells heavily of cologne.

"What do you have in your pants, son?" he asks.

Past his shoulder, out in the middle of the avenue, the policeman holds one hand over his heart and the other, open-palmed, alongside his face like the Sacred Heart statue on the landing between the first and second floors at Saints Peter and Paul.

• • •

Once during religion class back in sixth grade, Mickey fell asleep. Sister woke him by tugging him to his feet by a sideburn, and he was made to stand next to his desk, extend his arms horizontally and hold in each hand a Baltimore Catechism. She wouldn't even allow him to go to the lavatory. When, after considerable time, Mickey could no longer take the pain, he grunted and moaned. Sister ignored him and went on with Religion. Suddenly, Mickey began peeing. He just stood there, eyes closed, grunting through clenched teeth, arms shaking as he struggled to keep them outstretched, and let the water run out of him until it flowed from beneath his pants cuff and puddled at his feet. It kept coming and coming until it formed a little river that flowed along the not quite plumb floor to the north end of the room where Sister stood reading to us about rubber plantations.

Too shocked to even laugh, each of us stared at Mickey. When Sister looked up and saw that she no longer had our attention, she looked at Mickey, then down at the river, nearly at her black shoes. You could see that she didn't immediately get it because she kept glancing from Mickey to her feet. And then she did, her eyes bugging behind her wire glasses and the entire lower part of her face sliding down to her white bib.

Mickey started to laugh, harder and harder, but the rest of us, our eyes now on Sister, trying to unfreeze herself and pounce, were too scared to laugh. Mickey tried to stop laughing, but he couldn't. He never could. Sister dragged him—the Baltimore Catechisms flew out of his hands and landed in the urine—to the cloakroom. When they reappeared, a diaper had been rigged over Mickey's wet trousers and he wore a baby bonnet. His eyes were those of an assassin, but still he laughed. Sister marched him to the landing between floors where he was displayed all day at the foot of the Sacred Heart statue, one of Jesus's hands on his heart and the other up like a cop's halting traffic.

● ● ●

"What do you have in your pants?" the clerk asks again.

"I don't know," I say.

He turns and looks at the cop, and asks: "Would you like me to call that policeman?"

"No."

He locks the front door, then takes me gently by the arm, leads me into a little office crammed with opened cardboard boxes of records, and closes the door.

"I'll give you a choice, son. I'll either call your father or that policeman. It's up to you. But you better right now return what's in your pants."

I don't say anything.

"How's it going to go?" he asks.

I pull out the record and lay it on a cluttered, gray metal desk in the middle of which is a black telephone.

"I don't have a father," I say.

"Is there somebody you can call?"

"My mother."

He points at the phone. "Well, you better get on that phone right now and tell her to come down here and fetch you."

"She's at work."

"There's a telephone book under the phone."

I've never called Francene at work. It takes a while for her to come to the phone. Sears is only three blocks away, and she is there in minutes. I don't lift my head from the floor to look at her as the clerk relates what happened and turns me over to her. He claims he knows I'm a good boy, and that I'll never do such a thing again. We shake hands before Francene and I depart and, at her urging, I thank him.

Francene has an outrageous walk. Speed. Like a house afire. I never can keep up without jogging and today, under the circumstances, I let her outdistance me, but not so far that I can't hear those high heels clicking off the sidewalk, nosing her forward like a runner at the tape, foraging pigeons lifting up in her wake, her arms swinging, one of them strapped at the elbow crook with her handbag. The big coat, the hat under which her brown hair flows, pins and beads and earrings twinkling in the sun. Past Fashion Hosiery, the VFW, Alex Reich's, Gammon's Restaurant, where she'd often take me for pie and coffee, past black-stoned Eastminster Presbyterian with its high, narrow windows of apocalyptic stained glass. She has not yet said a word. When we get to Sears, I ask her if she's going back to work.

"No," she says, without turning, and I know it's going to be bad.

The instant we are in our apartment, she lights a cigarette, sits down at the telephone stand, tracks down a number in the phone book and dials.

"Is this Juvenile Court?" she says into the receiver. "Yes, my name is Francene Renzo, and I would like you to come and pick up my son."

I am standing right in front of her. For the first time since she walked into the Record Mart she looks at me. Her eyes are clear and brilliant, the color of ripe, bluish limes. She is not kidding. I have driven her to this.

"Please, Francene," I say, my eyes filling.

She lays her hand over the mouthpiece.

"Don't you dare cry. Don't you even dare. A boy old enough to thieve is too old to cry."

"Please." A tear rolls down my cheek.

"I don't even want to see that," she spits, smearing the tear from my cheek with her hand.

"Please."

"Please, what?"

"Don't send me away. I'm sorry."

Francene's expression suddenly changes, and she removes her hand from the mouthpiece. "Yes, I'm still here," she says into it.

Burying my face in her lap, I wail: "Please, Francene."

"Yes, may I call you back?" she says. "Thank you. Bye."

She hangs up, then stands so abruptly, I fall backwards to the floor. I have never seen her so worked up.

"Get up," she says, handing me a Kleenex from her purse, "and stop crying." She is still in her hat and coat.

"Last chance, Bobby. You understand? Next time I let them come and get you. No child of mine is going to be a common thief. Do you understand?"

"Yes."

"Do you know what it's like down there at Juvenile Court? It's crawling with rats and roaches. All you have to eat is bread and water and they beat you with rubber hoses. And if that doesn't work, they send you to Morganza or Thorn Hill and nobody ever hears about you again. Close your eyes. I want you to close your eyes and just imagine what it's like."

I close my eyes as commanded and find myself standing in front of the incinerator in the middle of Saints Peter and Paul schoolyard, its brick smokestack lurching into the clouds like a steeple, a black iron door built into the masonry. Behind it I hear muffled fire flapping and the sound of voices like those Mickey and I heard from the naked people telling secrets on the big screen beyond the doors leading into the theater the day we snuck into the lobby of the Cameraphone and stood there not knowing what to do. Incinerator voices just inside the black door. I open it. There sit Mickey, Boris Karloff, Peter Lorre, Lon Chaney, and Father Vita. Toasting pigeons stuck to the end of sticks, they recline on coals. Just above their heads, fire bounces off the incinerator walls.

"Welcome to Juvie," Father Vita says.

Francene's sucker punch, even though it knocks me to the linoleum, restores me to the temporal world. I gape up at her and see her right fist still balled. She opens it and reaches down to help me up. Never before has she struck me, not even the slightest tap.

"Are you all right, Bobby?" she asks in a way that makes me think maybe someone else hit me.

"Yes." My jaw still works, though a bit slowly.

"I had to do it. You don't have a father, and a spanking would have been an insult. I thought it would be better this way. I don't even know how to spank. I'll tell you one thing, though. You steal again and whatever you saw behind your eyes is what you wish on yourself. So help me, God, Bobby. Ever again, it's Juvenile Court. Then it won't be enough for you to just say 'Sorry.' I'll let them come after you."

I decide never to do anything wrong again, and if I forget for a moment, I can just look across the street at Platehead, a Pirates baseball cap plopped on his head, getting smaller and smaller, an aged kid with translucent onion skin, like one of the munchkins, his glowing eyes getting bigger and bigger, while the rest of him shrinks. That's what happens to bad kids.

CHAPTER 8

I suppose Mickey's death—he didn't last six months—
was inevitable. East Liberty high opera. Liturgical even.
There's a big show of trooping to the D'Andrea's, the women
sitting with Mrs. D'Andrea, in the first of the black dresses
she would wear for the next year, holding her hand, while
the men brood at the kitchen table and drink shots and beers.

I sit out on the porch with the other kids and stare at
the window in our kitchen from which I had stared at
Mickey. He is laid out for three nights at DeRosa's, and
every night after the funeral home closes at nine, everyone
gathers at the D'Andrea's and eats pans of lasagna and
eggplant and chicken cacciatore the neighborhood women
cook, all of it swimming in blood.

People say Mickey's death is all for the best. But looking
at Mrs. D'Andrea, her red, furzy hair, and penciled eyebrows
writhing on her powdered forehead as she sobs for four days,
it is not clear to me that it is for the best. On the fourth
day, I sing at the early Requiem and never shed a tear. By

ten in the morning, Mickey lies under a cope of sweet-smelling soil in Mount Carmel Cemetery, the twelve gray gloves on top of his coffin where they are thrown by the pallbearers. Father Vita, still in his black vestments, walks down the hill to the limousine, and Mrs. D'Andrea faints. Once home Francene rips off her black lace mantilla, lies down on her bed and sleeps for hours, while terrified I hover at her bedside watching her breathe. Slower and fainter until I convince myself that she's entered some enchanted state from which she'll never wake save for my father's spellbreaking kiss. When I can't stand it another second, I wake her to say that it's getting dark outside.

We sit on the living room floor and eat Chef Boy-ar-dee canned ravioli cold out of the can, toast and pistachios, while watching *The Sands of Iwo Jima*. It's the best movie I've ever seen. Francene tells me I can never be a soldier. She doesn't like John Wayne; she says he's a show-off. He's my favorite actor. But at the end a sniper kills him in a foxhole and I can't shake it for days. It's like seeing someone I love die. That's silly, Francene says. It's just a movie.

After a while people stop looking on the D'Andrea's porch for Platehead, and for the moment I have nothing to remind me of what happens to bad kids. Baseball season finally arrives. In my first pack of baseball cards, I get Roy Face and Bob Friend, both Pirates, and I figure the hard times are over. Maybe Mickey's death *is* for the best. It's a relief to not always have to look at him. For Lent I give up movies and spend almost all my time playing ball, fooling around with my baseball cards, and staying out of the Hollow, which has become increasingly dangerous because of the Jets and packs of black kids from the projects.

During Holy Week I break down and go to Confession. Father Vita, as usual, calls me by name throughout, completely unnerving me. I very much need that well-preserved charade of anonymity. What I tell him—or rather what I convince myself I'm telling him—is that I'm being haunted by Mickey, that I need to be relieved of my guilt over betraying him. I relate the whole story of how Mickey had been flailed so unmercifully, how he had stood the beating and even laughed, but was so hurt that I had betrayed him that he had wept in front of me. How because of this I feel his death is somehow my fault. I spill it all, every bit of it.

Father says nothing more than "Mmmm-hmmm" and "Uh-huh," the entire time, which I find reassuring. From outside the confessional, I hear coughs and shuffles, and imagine the line outside my box queuing all the way down Larimer Avenue. The whole time I am in there, I think about the plate in Mickey's head, like the white chipped ones on Isaly's steam table, with the green piping around the outside rim, how after a hundred years, all that will be left in Mount Carmel of Mickey will be a dish, on the bottom of which is stamped in calligraphy: *Caribe China, Puerto Rico, U.S.A, E-3.*

I realize I have been smelling Vick's Vapo-rub which Mickey always reeked of after his accident. His mother was so afraid of pneumonia that she kept his chest smeared with it. Peering through the little screen separating me from Father Vita, I see the profile of a spindly paralytic wearing the confessor's stole, his tongue slapping out of his mouth like a baby carp and a baseball hat on his tiny head.

"For your penance," he says, in his gargling, underwater voice, "Beat yourself." Then Mickey vanishes, and it's Father Vita again, saying, as usual, "Say three Our Fathers and three Hail Marys."

In truth, I haven't told him a thing about Mickey, just the same old formulaic list of venial sins guaranteed to score three Our Fathers and three Hail Marys and a spotless soul. I say an Act of Contrition, accept Father's blessing, and walk out of the confessional to a gang of wizened penitents who read me like tarot. I forsake the altar rail and my appointed penance. I'm headed for the Hollow. Mickey is getting even with me, but I don't care.

I beat it out the side entrance, next to the rectory, and run down the walk towards Larimer Avenue. Standing there, as if he has been waiting for me, is Nino, the Luccettis' dog. He is the color of a grocery bag and weighs as much as a good-sized man. I try to run back into church, but he is instantly upon me, knocking me down, and fastening his jaws around one of my ankles. I plead and fight, I call him by name, but he is too big and strong. Two old ladies screech at him in Italian. *Arresto.* Hearing them, Father Guissino, the ancient, retired pastor, looks up from his iris bed on the rectory lawn and crabs off after us. But Nino, with me in his mouth, is already well past him.

The dog waits for traffic to clear, then crosses to the other side of Larimer, loping along the sidewalk toward Cici's store where I buy baseball cards and where my grandfather had the stroke that killed him. Cici is a tall, skinny bald man who looks just like Jimmy Durante. When he sees what is happening to me, he flies out of his store after us as we whiz by.

Nino darts into Booze Alley, so named because of the spray-painted legend across a boarded window of one of the abandoned buildings that lines the alley. It is paved with red cobblestones, smoothed by the timeless tread of drunks, and grouted with broken bottle dust.

I have no feeling in my ankle, only the sense of wetness. From the moment he seized me, I have spoken to him, calling him by name, begging him to stop, trying to remain calm; but I have a premonition that he will never let me go.

He tows me out of the alley and onto Omega Street. Nonna, on her hands and knees, in her black widow's frock, grinds away at the sidewalk in front of her house with cleanser and a scrub brush. A gray, soapy scum foams about her. Even her skin has turned black. She has warned me about this *cane*, Nino, many times.

"Nonna," I yell. I am afraid she won't recognize me; it has been so long since we've seen each other.

Getting to her feet, she fetches her broom standing against the porch, and as Nino trots past her she beats his flanks with it. He doesn't seem to mind this at all. He stops and stares at her. As she beats him, she screams, "*Basto. Basto.*" Enough.

Hanging limply from Nino's muzzle, I figure I am dreaming, or at least in a movie. Except for the black rag, instead of a pointed hat, Nonna, with that broom and her black outfit, looks like Margaret Hamilton in *The Wizard of Oz*. When Nino starts off again, Nonna drops her broom, throws herself on me, and holds fast to one of my arms. Undaunted, dragging both of us, he inches his way along the sidewalk.

Cici, waving a pistol, finally emerges from Booze Alley with Father Guissino tottering behind. Cici slips alongside us and takes aim. His hand shakes. He brings his other hand up to steady the gun.

"Please," Nonna shrieks, "please."

"I can't do it," Cici says.

"Shoot," croaks Father Giussino.

"I can't," Cici repeats, handing him the gun. "You must do it, Father."

"*Jesu Christe*," sobs Nonna.

I gaze up at the beautiful blue sky and try to remember my penance from Father Vita. I no longer have feeling in my leg. My clothes are in tatters. Nino halts and turns his head toward the priest. Father Guissino's extended arm quivers. At the first report, Nonna lets go of my arm. Father Guissino, nearly on top of the dog, fires twice more; then he lurches exhaustedly against Cici. The two old men fall to the ground. Nino, for an instant, eyes them and Nonna; then, with me flopping from his mouth, gallops away.

• • •

I wake up lying on a big, black, flat rock in the middle of one of the Hollow's crabapple groves. For some seconds, staring through the pink apple blossoms at the high, cloud-powdered cobalt sky and waves of sparrows diving in and out of the branches, I'm unable to quit the dream about Nino, and I forget what I am doing in the Hollow in the first place. Then I remember Mickey. It is nearly quiet, except for the occasional whoosh of boulevard traffic and birds calling. I want to sleep, but am afraid I'll stray back into nightmare.

I reach for one of the green, elastic sumac branches dangling in my face. It comes away cleanly from the spindly trunk, a dab of milky sap that smells like wet sheets falling from it. I strip it of its leaves with one quick swipe and then whip it about. As it cuts the air, it sings with electricity.

Taking off my shirt, I sit cross-legged. The sun angles directly down upon me; the wind is warm. Twenty lashes I have decided is a fitting penance. Ten with my right hand over my left shoulder, then ten with my left over my right shoulder. By the fourth I am in pain, but I am determined to square things with Mickey. In my head he smiles as Sister's board clips him again and again, his innocent head of hair like a bird with a broken wing trying to fly. At the end of my hand, the sumac fizzes. I imagine my back crosshatched with bloody gashes like flogging victims in the movies. After twenty, I simply sit there, my back as if crawling with bloodsuckers. But I feel better, and finally I put my shirt back on, keel over on my side, my face against the cool rock, and fall asleep again.

● ● ●

Nonna swears there are dreams from which people never wake, that *Satana* reads vagrant minds and can tell when the time is right to filch a soul. Sown into her night garments are rosaries and holy medals. She sleeps with a crucifix and sprinkles her bed every night with holy water. Above all, no matter the season, she props wide her night windows because the devil, afraid of heights, will not venture into an upstairs room with an open window.

Unsure whether I am awake or asleep, I hear what sounds like footsteps, heavy and dragging. The crack of

undergrowth. I pull Uncle John's letter opener from my
dungarees pocket.

Spacaluccio looks like a kangaroo, Nonna says. *Canguro*,
with the head of a man, a man's trousers and brogans, and
the hairy bare breast of the beast. He searches the Hollow
for something he has lost, but no one knows what it is; nor
could he, deprived of speech, say himself. Perhaps one of
his eyes. He possesses but one, huge and sooty. The other
he has sewn shut himself with a tailor's whipstitch. Perhaps
he is in search of his own child. And that is why he devours
disobedient children. Because his *bambino* disobeyed and
strayed into the Hollow and drowned, a thousand years ago
when it was still under water. Out of his little body sprouted
the sumac that now chokes the Hollow. Under the bridge
deck, wrapped like aging salamis, the monster's cache of
captured, dead children hang in the rafters.

Spacaluccio, a peasant from Foggia, working as a riveter
when the bridge was first constructed, fell off a girder, down
and down, into an abutment footer of freshly poured
concrete where he was buried alive, forever interred, unable
to rest until receiving the proper rites and funeral.

He was a soldier who came back from war only to find
his young wife had run off with the huckster, his grief such
that he hurled himself off the bridge. At night he wanders,
terrorizing the Hollow lovers, searching for his bride.

Without smiling, without softening, Nonna tells me

all of these stories, and I wonder how they can all be. Yet she, and Francene even, seems living proof that in all of us several monsters reside. What one must do upon meeting, God forbid, Spacaluccio, Nonna advises—and here she brings my forehead to hers, garlic and parsley sauteing in her mouth—is to make the *faccia contento*. He may not hurt you or steal from you if you are happy. So you must put on the face of happiness. For your unhappiness, he will eat you. If all else fails, one should smile broadly, or even laugh, if possible, and say his name aloud three times. Nonna laughs, something she doesn't do often and pats my cheeks.

"How do you become happy, Nonna?"

At this question, she grows morose, her eyes instantly spilling tears, and says, "You must not live if you wish to be happy." Then she kneels and drives me to my knees beside her. "Let us say the rosary for Spacaluccio."

Francene declares Spacaluccio just a story made up by crazy Italians to scare their children. They are in love with misery. It is their genius, and out of it they conjure a monster. They, really, are the monsters. East Liberty is a monster. Its enemy is happiness; it eats children. In fact, East Liberty and Spacaluccio are the same things. Francene doesn't believe in him, but I do. If people can put the eyes on you and make a tree grow inside your heart, if your mouth can freeze into an idiot's if you make an unkind face at your elders, if your arm can turn to stone and stick out of your grave if you ever hit your mother, then why can't there be a monster living under the Hollow bridge?

• • •

I am wide awake. Something makes its way toward me. Spacaluccio. What else could it be ripping through the bramble and heaving like a furnace? My back burning, I scramble into a thicket of burdock. It is the Jets. Dominic Fusca, himself, a BB gun jammed into the waist of his pants; and his lieutenant, Butters, a petty, mean vandal with a pushed-in face of acne and greasy bangs, a gun in his pants too. Two orangish-blonde girls, close enough in looks to be twins, carry between them a pole with dead squirrels strung to it. One of them has a transistor radio. I hear drums and Lou Christie's falsetto, but I can't make out the words. At the tail of this procession are four other boys, uniform in their T-shirts, slicked-back hair and doped-looking, cigarette-smoking scowls.

The last of them holds a rope tethered around the neck of a black kid wearing a red jersey, his hands trussed behind him. He walks deliberately, eyes straight ahead, his nose bleeding. They tie him to a tree just to the left of me, then build a fire in a small clearing by the creek.

The Jets sit around the fire, smoking cigarettes, passing a big jug of red wine, and feeding the flames. With switchblades, the blondes cut the squirrels off the pole, climb up on the black rock and slice them chin to loin; then, chatting the whole time, reach in with their bare hands and scoop out the guts and pile them on the rock. Slicing around the head and neck, they little by little coax the pelts off the way I've seen Francene peel off her stockings. The tails they cut off and carefully arrange in their belts, but they leave the heads, fur and all, on the carcasses. Were it not for that, I would mistake them for newborn babies.

On their way to the creek to rinse the squirrels, they walk right by me, so close I smell perfume, and see on one of them a Peabody High School class ring grouted with blood. As they pass the black boy, they giggle.

The Jets get louder and louder. I feel the heat of the fire. The blondes return with the squirrels on spits, take seats, and hold them over the fire. Instantly the heads burst into flame, the fur crackling. Fusca grabs the spits from the blondes and capers over to the black kid. He dances and whoops and waves the flaming squirrels in his face, then stops and laughs until he doubles over. The others have gotten to their feet to watch. They laugh too. A couple of them can barely stand. Fusca stumbles back to the fire, the heads sending up stinking black smoke, and sits heavily.

"Cook these goddam things," he says, handing the squirrels to one of the blondes, then pulls her hard against him and kisses her.

Butters pulls out his pistol and takes a shot across the clearing at the black kid. I jump. The sparrows roosted in the apple trees keen, then lift up in black shadows. Butters shoots several times into them and one falls, still alive, into the bushes above my head where it flutters madly. Butters again levels the pistol at the black kid who makes a noise like humming.

"Let's eat first," Fusca says.

It is getting dark. I am not sure what I am more afraid of: the Jets, or being caught in the Hollow at nightfall. The cars, wandering across the huge, levitating bridge, are barely visible. I don't know if they are going to shoot the black kid or roast him over the fire. For all I know they'll eat him—and me too. Maybe they'll just leave him for Spacaluccio to feast on.

A song I really like comes on the radio.

"Turn that up," says Fusca.

The radio belts: "Ladybug, silver dollar, rabbit's foot, and a pink carnation and a horseshoe."

They all get to their feet and dance and sing in the firelight. I creep out of the bush—the wounded bird still fluttering— and crawl along the edge of the apple trees and sumac until I come up behind the tree the kid is trussed to. There is still enough light to see that they have tied him with bakery string from Stagno's, wrapped dozens and dozens of times around his wrist and then around the tree. He still has that rope around his neck. Maybe they plan to hang him.

"Don't make a sound. I'm a friend," I say, stealing my lines from any number of movies, especially westerns, where the soon-to-be-tortured are saved from the whiskey-crazed Indians, cavorting around the fire, by the exact rescue I am performing. With my letter opener I saw away, but the going, strand by strand, is slow. The string is wet with blood. The entire tree shakes with the kid's trembling, and I can feel within him as I cut a little song of terror.

The Jets gyrate around the fire as the song winds down. Finally I cut all the way through, he is free, and we hustle off through the undergrowth. Suddenly the music goes dead, and the only noise in the woods is our thrashing. We hear for a moment their voices, raised and angry, and then they are after us. In what is left of the light, trees and bushes and trash are mere silhouettes fading quickly into invisibility. We crash into things, our limbs and faces switched by the dense foliage. But, hearing the cough and twang of those BB guns firing, we never stop. At one point the black kid cries out and I know he's been shot.

There is a swampy spot I know about just after crossing under the bridge where a discarded doorjamb, door and all, wedges into a stand of stunted larches choked with catbriar. When we get to it, I open the door and we step through it. On the other side is a shortcut up to Moga Street where we'll be safe. But it is almost straight up and down. Over the years, concrete trucks, at the end of the day, have pulled into Moga, a dead end, and dumped into the Hollow the concrete that hadn't been used. The concrete has set up in odd ways, around trees and bushes and dumped washers, dryers, sinks, couches, automobile chassis, innumerable tires and miscellaneous trash so that the cliff connecting Moga to the Hollow resembles a huge outlandish sculpture.

I have climbed it before, but never in the dark. Once we reach the top, exhausted and so beat up from everything that has happened, we stagger into Paul Pagano's backyard and collapse. Paul is a cement finisher, and he and his wife, Minnie, are old friends of my mother. I like Paul a lot. He is a tough guy without being a jerk, and Francene once told me he and my father had been good friends. Even if the Jets have tracked us, they know better than to come into his yard.

The black kid and I lay at the base of a brick grotto Paul built for the Blessed Virgin, with a lightbulb above her head that stays on all night. Mary, so beautiful, in flowing blue robes, her hands held out in absolute understanding, and beneath her bare feet the squashed *serpente*.

In that little bit of light I see that the kid is a man, and not a particularly young one. He has a clipped little mustache in the patch just under his nose, and gray in his hair. I guess he figures I have known all along, but to me it's a revelation, as if he has rescued me. If the Jets ever find out that I am the one, I'll be more than sorry, but it seems worth it.

We walk out onto Saint Marie Street. Paul lives just three houses from the Hollow Bridge which crosses Meadow Street and leads ultimately into the heart of the black neighborhoods. The only words I hear this man speak all night are "Thank you, son" as we shake hands there at the edge of Spacaluccio's hideout. I watch him walk the bridge until he disappears into complete darkness on the other side. Then I start running home. I am very, very late, and Francene is going to kill me.

CHAPTER 9

For my thirteenth birthday, Francene takes me to dinner at Minutello's on Shady Avenue. She asks me if I want to invite along a friend, but I don't really have those kinds of friends. I think it would be nice to invite Nonna, but she and Francene aren't really speaking, and I haven't seen her in a long time. Besides she doesn't believe in restaurants.

My Aunt Lena waitresses at Minutello's. We get a table in the bar so she can wait on us. She wears a black jumper over a white shirt with a black necktie, and her puffy gray hair in a black net. Her mouth, rarely without a cigarette— she perpetually has one burning in an ashtray on the bar—except when she is waiting on a table, stretches across her face, and her flat nose almost touches her upper lip. She seems too old to still be working. She is really an adopted aunt; and I call her husband, who looks like a happy John Carradine with a crewcut, Uncle Abe.

They live on McDonald Street, on the back end of Larimer Field, in a strange little pillbox house entered by descending a flight of stairs off the street. I see them only occasionally, mostly on holidays. One Christmas Day I accidentally strangled one of their cat's newborn, snow-white kittens by putting a rope around its neck so I could take it for a walk. For the rest of our visit, Uncle Abe played with and talked to the dead kitten, even had it do little dances, pretending it was still alive for my benefit. They never had kids.

When Francene was pregnant with me, she rented a second floor apartment from Uncle Abe and Aunt Lena on Auburn Street. She lived on seven dollars a week unemployment. They told her to forget about the rent until after I was born. I don't know if my father was even in the picture at the time. Because of him, my grandparents had, for the time being, disowned Francene. Then winter came and it snowed every day from December to March. The city was mired in white. Nobody went anywhere, and I was due. Francene baked bread and bought produce from the huckster. Aunt Lena sent supper up regularly, and once a week Uncle Abe brought Francene a twenty-cent pie. It cost a hundred and ten dollars to have a baby, nine months care and delivery, calcium and vitamin pills. At the time, my mother didn't have that kind of money. Uncle Abe and Aunt Lena took care of everything. They even bought a bassinet and dresser for me.

The night Francene went into labor, there was a blizzard.

Twenty-four inches on the ground before she decided to call a cab. But the cabs weren't running and neither were the streetcars. All the ambulances were tied up or snowbound. Uncle Abe was working shifts at J & L Steel and happened to be home. Aunt Lena woke him and together they shoveled the snow away from the tires of their car so he could put chains on. But it took too long, and the jack kept slipping on the ice. As she watched in increasing pain from the porch, Francene's water broke. It ran hotly down her legs, hissed and steamed in the snow, then froze into a white, crystal amnion.

Uncle Abe fetched a child's sled from the basement and Francene was bundled onto it. Together Uncle Abe and Aunt Lena shoveled through the walls of snow and drayed her by sled the half mile or so to the hospital. It must have taken them hours. By the time they got there it was too late to anesthetize my mother. She was rushed up to delivery where she birthed me within ten minutes of entering the hospital, a floor-length mirror stationed at her feet so she could watch my surreal burst into the world. Francene asked Uncle Abe and Aunt Lena to be my godparents.

Aunt Lena hugs and kisses me and tells me to stand up, then raves over how tall I'm growing. When Francene tells her it's my thirteenth birthday, she kisses me some more, and introduces us to the other waitresses and the bartender, telling them that I'm her godchild and today is my birthday.

"How's Abe, Lena?" Francene asks.

Aunt Lena puts her hands out in front of her and moves them up and down slightly as if gauging which one is heavier.

"You know, honey, *mezza-mezza*. Good days and bad days. He has to wear that oxygen thing all the time now. God bless him, though, he's got a hard head. He does all right for himself. Never a complaint. You know him. What a kidder. Still has a little garden, a few tomatoes and peppers, still goes down to the clubyard and plays bocce on Sundays. I can't get him to quit the cigarettes, though." Her voice is pure nasal. Mae West.

"That's so dangerous with that oxygen," Francene says.

"I tell him. You're going to blow us up one of these days. Either that or the blacks will. It's starting to get bad down there. Everybody's moving to the suburbs. But where are we going, me and Abey? We're too old to move. And our house is paid for."

"When are you going to retire, Lena?"

"Honey, I can't afford to. You know, Abey had to leave the mill early because of his health, so he doesn't get near the pension he would have if he had stuck it out till sixty-five. I just thank God I can get up every day and go to work."

"Well, you sure look good."

"Honey, there's nothing I can do about that." She laughs a raspy, smoker's laugh, and we laugh too.

"You." She looks at me, and waves her finger. "You stay in school and make something of yourself and take care of your mother. He's a handsome boy, Francene. God love him. Just me and Abey like two straphangers. No kids to look in on us. But what are you going to do? The dear Lord does what he sees fit and, really, He's been good to us. This one. I can't believe he's thirteen. My God, the day you were born. It was like the North Pole. Ask your mother."

She pulls a pad and pen out of her jumper pocket. "Now what can I get you?"

I order veal parmigiana, and Francene a giant antipasto. Aunt Lena brings out a platter of linguine with red clam sauce on the house. Francene slides an envelope across the table. Inside is a five-dollar bill and a little booklet entitled *All About Birthdays: Thoughts on Growing Up by the Peanuts Characters*. On the cover a typically doleful Charlie Brown sits on a bench next to a birthday cake with a piece missing and one lit candle; he eats the missing wedge. I leaf through it and smile. On each page, after "It's easy to tell you're growing up when . . ." is a scene with the Peanuts characters and a phrase that completes the sentence like "the crowd is always one dance ahead of you," and "when you realize that all your dreams of glory won't come true." Francene loves Peanuts, which I can't figure out. The booklet is signed

Love, Mama, even though I never call Francene anything but Francene. She calls Nonna *Mama*. This confuses me a little, but I don't say anything except "Thanks, Francene" because she's having a good time. When she comes to an olive, or anchovy, or an artichoke heart, she forks it onto my plate. I think about what Aunt Lena said, and how some day it will fall to me to take care of Francene. I think too of Nonna, how we never see her.

Francene wants to talk about my Confirmation, coming up in May. What name am I going to take? Who's going to be my sponsor? Should we have a party? She wants me to take the name Luigi because that was my grandfather's name, but I hate that name. It is a name people will make fun of, but what can I tell her? That I won't honor the name of her dead father? She says that if Luigi seems a little too strong, I can take Louis, which is its American equivalent. But I don't like Louis either. She's so animated and happy. I end up saying, sure, of course, I'll take Luigi or Louis, whichever she thinks best.

I can't think of a person in the world who can be my sponsor, except my grandfather, and he is dead. A party sounds like fun, but who will we invite? I don't even know why we are talking about this. I suddenly feel like I have a ton on my mind. Confirmation is the manhood ritual of the church where one becomes a soldier in the Army of Christ.

For weeks I have been studying a list of questions that Sister has assured us the Bishop will ask at random during the ceremony: Summarize Pope Pius XII's 1950 encyclical, *Humani Generis*; What are the spiritual and corporal works of mercy?; Name the individual parts of the Mass; and a dozen more. Right there in front of the entire congregation. I don't at all feel up to being a man.

In a year, I'll be in high school. The nuns still have me figured for a priest and want me to go right into seminary. There is a boarding school in Cleveland, Saint Charles Borromeo, where Father Vita has connections. My grades are superior. If I do okay on the entrance test—and taking into account my "homelife," as it is referred to by the sisters and Father Vita—he thinks I have a good shot at a scholarship. I don't get it. It's like I am an orphan or something and have no say in the matter. Yet I never level with them about how I feel. It isn't just that I don't want to be a priest; I can't be a priest. Besides I'd never leave Francene. But I've never said a word to her about any of this. If I end up with a scholarship to a seminary in Cleveland, she'll be the last to know.

• • •

At least one day a week after school, I go to the convent and do chores: trim hedges, wash windows, clean out flower beds, whatever the sisters ask me to do. I love being in the lavish gardens scrolled with stone walks winding among birdhouses, fountains, beds of daffodils and tulips, trellises of climbing roses, painted statues of Saints Anthony, Francis, Joseph, and Madonna after Madonna, the golden-haired Christ-children, sweet and worried.

In a circle, enclosing the gardens, tower fourteen junipers to which are affixed the fourteen Stations of the Cross. The ancient nuns, too old to teach, or simply, as some say, "too tired," move whispering in the shadow of those trees while the crows scold them from the high branches.

After finishing my work, I am led down a long, marble corridor of identical rooms and given a snack in the kitchen, an enormous white-tile and chrome vault ringed with hanging pots and pans. Usually a piece of cake or pie that the nuns have baked and a glass of milk which I consume with Sister hovering over me and smiling, asking me questions about what my life at home is like, dishing up another piece of pie. At these times, I wonder myself what my life is like, and it never occurs to me that I am being interrogated. I am sure that I like my life, and I tell Sister this; that I love baseball and Francene and that we stay up and watch old movies and eat whatever we want whenever we want.

Sister asks me if I love God. I tell her "Yes," but I am not really sure that I believe in God. She then asks me if Francene ever hits me. Francene smacked me in the jaw that one time after the Record Mart, and that is it; but I'm not about to get into this, so I just say "No." Considering the way she used to demolish Mickey, it seems peculiar that Sister is suddenly so sensitive about kids getting banged around.

I know she wants to ask about my father, but I no longer think much about that whole issue. It's just there, like Mickey on his porch day after day. Having no father is just part of the scenery.

Sister asks me if I really want to be a priest. What I want is for this charade to be over, but I don't want to part with the tidy, starched and gleaming world it affords me.

"Yes, Sister," I say, looking into her earnest, bespectacled, birdlike face. She squeezes my hand and nods, as if at that moment we've both happened on something mystical.

Sitting there one day in that very pose, we hear shouting and then in upon us bursts a nun, still in wimple, but clothed only in black brassiere and underpants. She stops to regard us, folding her hands on her bare belly. Her chestnut hair has worked its way out of the veil, a strand of it falling across one of her blue eyes, down across her slight, freckled nose. She is barefoot, the skin of her arms and shoulders unearthly pale against the black cloth, gone to gooseflesh in the chill kitchen, the fine hair of her arms standing straight, attracting the fragmented sun trapped in the room. She looks so very young, no older than I, it seems. Almost as if we know each other, we cannot take our eyes off each other. Several nuns storm in and grab her. Spitting and kicking and hissing as they wrangle her out of the room, she howls like an animal.

Sister, obviously upset, says, "You'd better go home now, Roberto. I'm terribly, terribly sorry that you had to see that. Sister Bibiana is not well at all."

Walking home, thinking about the mad nun standing there in front of me in the convent kitchen, I realize beyond a shadow of a doubt that I'll never be a priest.

• • •

Francene looks like a kid sometimes. With her head cocked to the side, her mouth half open as she chews, and a funny little grin that accentuates her overbite, she moves her plate to the edge of the table.

"What are you doing?" I ask.

"Reading the place mat."

Minutello's place mats are maps of Italy.

"I just glanced down and saw Bologna." She giggles.

"What?"

"Bologna is Angolob backwards. *Angolob*." She laughs out loud.

I move my plate off the place mat and see Rome. "What about Emor?"

Francene, one eye squinted, looks at me for a moment.

"Emor. Emor. Oh, Emor. Yes. Yes. I've always wanted to travel to Emor."

"All roads lead to Emor," I say.

"Selpan is nice, too. Nonno and Nonna were born in Selpan."

"Do we still have relatives in Selpan?"

"Yes, we do."

"Let's go to Selpan."

"And as long as we're there, we can visit Ecnerolf and Nalim."

We laugh and laugh until the other people in the bar turn to look at us. Aunt Lena waltzes up to our table holding a cheesecake with thirteen burning candles, and the whole bar sings "Happy Birthday" to me.

EAST LIBERTY

CHAPTER 10

My favorite baseball player is Bill Mazeroski, the Pirates' second basemen. William Stanley Mazeroski. Of Polish-Catholic ancestry. Son of a West Virginia coal miner. Not a big guy, but strong, regular-looking, though on my favorite baseball card of him—from the 1961 Topps series, which I have enshrined in my head as his official portrait—he models movie star good looks. Montgomery Clift. His beautiful wife's name is Milene. He wears number 9. His nickname is "No-touch" because on his double play pivot, his reception from the shortstop and relay to the first baseman is so seamless that he creates the optical illusion of never having touched the ball. He bats eighth and is, really, a humble guy who never gets credit for how revolutionary he is.

In 1958 he hit nineteen homers, and he hit the home run in the bottom of the ninth in the seventh game of the 1960 World Series that beat the unbeatable New York Yankees. I copy every move and gesture of his, keep a wad of bubble gum in my cheek for tobacco when I'm playing, magic-marker 9s on the backs of my T-shirts, and, even though Francene wants me to take for Confirmation the name of Nonno, my first choice is Stanley, after Maz. I figure that if Jesus had played baseball he would have batted eighth and played second base.

• • •

In the fall of 1960 even the nuns, along with all the little Catholic children, like me, wear Kennedy buttons. It is a strange autumn. Along with the fear that if a Papist is elected president the Pontiff will move into the White House, there is a plague of suicidal squirrels. They fall out of trees and, as they scurry along electrical wires, inexplicably tumble to the pavement. They throw themselves under automobile tires. Dead animal collection works overtime. But nothing is stranger than the fact that the Pittsburgh Pirates compete in a World Series for the first time since 1927.

On Thursday, October 13, 1960, I have to step over dozens of dead squirrels, smashed and bloody, as I walk four and a half miles to make it to Forbes Field in time for Maz's at bat in the bottom of the ninth of the seventh game of the World Series.

After kneeling and kissing the plinth on which the statue of Honus Wagner stands just beyond the left field wall, I walk for the first time in my life into Forbes Field from the Sennott Street entrance, right up the ramp on the third base side, down to the rail and stand there staring at the expanse of grass like no other green I have ever seen, the blond infield dirt like no other dirt, the bases lovely and white, the distant green and ivy-covered walls and the flag lifting and falling. The players, icon-like and mendicant in their beautiful uniforms, move in slow motion.

The score is 9-9. Ralph Terry, number 32, is the Yankees' fifth pitcher of the day. Afflicted by uncharacteristic insomnia, he hadn't slept at all the night before, but had left the William Penn Hotel to wander the abandoned downtown streets of Pittsburgh, eating hamburgers at The White Tower and finally ending his night with a ride on the Duquesne Incline. Standing on an observation deck on Mount Washington, he had watched the sun come up on the Golden Triangle, the three great rivers coming omnisciently together. The top of the Gulf Building glowed red, predicting a warm, fair day for the decisive 1:05 game later that day. He was thankful he wouldn't have to pitch.

Maz gets off his knee in the on-deck circle, stumps to the plate, bends and scoops a handful of dirt to rub on his bat handle, shifts his tobacco cud from one cheek to the other and spits. He feels rested. The evening before, after oiling his glove and tightening a few seams, he had a bowl of corn flakes and then slept peacefully all night next to

Milene. He's not the superstitious type, but he said a rosary on his way to the park.

The first pitch is a high slider that gets away from Terry. For a moment he has a vision of Maz hitting it out, but he lays off it and the ump calls it a ball. Maz peers out at Terry whose face is nimbused by the late afternoon sun. The pin of the Kennedy button he wears beneath his flannels pricks him. He is about to motion for time when Terry gyres into his windup. Maz expects a breaking ball. The pitch sails in just under the letters, a tad inside. He waits and waits for the ball to break, but it never does.

Terry tries to call the pitch back, but all he really desires is sleep. Johnny Blanchard, the Yankee catcher, attempts, like a magician, to make the pitch disappear into his mitt, but Maz at the last second swings and hits it.

The ball, directly above Cletis Boyer's head at shortstop, is barely out of the infield when Yogi Berra, in left field, flicks down his sunglasses, takes a quarter turn to his left and then freezes. He hears church bells ringing all over Pittsburgh. The monstrous square Longine's clock sitting atop the green scoreboard in left stalls forever at 3:36.30. The three pigeons roosting on it never move, yet very visibly turn their heads in unison to watch the ball clear the wall, bounce into the open window of an abandoned stolen Nash in Schenley Park which is later towed to a Swissvale junkyard and pancaked. Bill Mazeroski is twenty-four years old. Like a holy man, I have all along known what was going to happen.

But the truth is, the real truth—if there is such a thing—is that I am not there at all. I witness Maz hit that homer, but not while standing along the third base line at Forbes Field. I've never been to Forbes Field. I run all the way home from school and get there just in time to see it on television.

The city goes berserk. People stay up all night singing and dancing under a sky raining paper and confetti that piles like snowdrifts and blocks traffic in and out of the city. Well past midnight, standing with Francene on the corner of Penn and Highland, watching people beat on pots and pans and set off cherry bombs, I've never seen such unadulterated happiness.

Yet as time goes on I begin, for some reason, insisting I am one of the 36,633 privileged citizens who had seen in person Maz's homer. It is a lie I tell first to myself and then to others, and I'm sure they know I'm lying, but indulge me nonetheless. Not only do I begin to believe it, but to invest it with a mythos that sometimes gets the better of me. I make up stories about it. Like a hallucination. For days and days the newspapers fill with World Series stories and photographs. Maz becomes, for a little while, more important than Jesus and Kennedy combined.

One of the classic pictures, published again and again, and overnight hung like an icon in black-and-white on walls all over Pittsburgh, is of Maz prancing down the third base line on his way to the plate after the homer. His right arm is up in the air, in his left his hardhat held out in front of him. Waiting for him is a mob of other Pirates, and at the fringe of the image the crowd stampedes out of the stands. Running maybe two yards behind him is a boy— his likeness is captured flawlessly—wearing a navy blazer with the emblem of Saints Peter and Paul on the breast pocket, a white shirt and navy tie. His hair is combed back; beneath the white walls, the ears are jugged, the eyes and heavy brow dark. In a full-out sprint he seems breathless, his hand reaching out as if all he wants is to touch Mazeroski. Indisputably, it is me. My face. My clothes. My outstretched hand. I imagine this not only the most perfect moment in Maz's life, but the most perfect moment in my life, too. But I wasn't there.

We invent ourselves and, like Mickey says, "It's all about art." What I wish for, more than anything else, is to have Bill Mazeroski for my father, for Milene to be my mother, to join that perfect family I see pictures of every year in the *Pirates Yearbook*. In late winter I would accompany my family to Fort Myers for spring training. Then until the weather chilled again, I'd travel the country watching my father play second base like no other man has ever done. In front of all of Pittsburgh, I would step into the Forbes Field infield wearing hometown black-and-gold flannels and play in the

Pirates' annual Father-Son game. Every year I'd see myself beaming in the *Yearbook*, an arm curled around my adoring mother's waist, my smiling, immortal father's hand tousling my hair.

• • •

I never have a chance to use the black bat. Before I even get to hit, on the game's first pitch, Poe cracks it against the ball he stole at Sears. I hadn't wanted anyone to so much as touch it until I had had that perfect swing I imagined. The crack is a hairline along the handle that can be easily fixed. A nail or two and a good tape job. I pick it up and lean it against my bike, then dig in and play ball. But I can't help being unhappy, my payback for stealing.

After the game, everyone spreads out to eat lunch on the grass just beyond second base. Since I have no lunch, Poe gives me half a baloney sandwich and a banana, and I get water from the fountain. A couple packs of Kools circulate and everyone, including me, takes one. I have smoked before, but I've never much cared for it. If I can just get home, everything will be all right. Better. Because of the bat I've really learned my lesson this time; I'll never do anything wrong again. Maybe all along God intended me to steal the bat, and have it broken, so that I can be restored through sorrow. There are plenty of stories of guys in the Bible who have to be jagoffs for a while before they can be saints. But I have to make it through this day. That is the pact I make with myself.

Freddy Cortino pulls a pack of playing cards out of his pants. Stripped and bloody women performing the most implausible, bestial acts. It is too much for me. Dizzy and nauseous, I look around the gorgeous, emerald grass and see strangers, much older than I, laughing as they gape at the cards; and I realize again that I am not one of them, or one of anyone, not even myself. That I do not have the ballast at that moment to keep from floating off into the sky.

"You know about girls?" Poe asks.

I can't see his eyes behind the sunglasses, but I know he is talking to me. Smoke wafts out of his mouth and he sucks it back in through his nostrils, his tongue out, the broken tooth flashing. I drag on my cigarette. Too deeply. The menthol stings. I begin to cough, and everyone laughs.

Poe removes his glasses. He turns his eyelids inside out and looks straight at me. The rest of them watch me. Not smiling, he repeats, "You know about girls?"

The inside of his eyelids are pink and wet. I can't stand to look at them.

"Yeah," I say.

They all laugh.

"You know what to do with them?" Poe asks.

He gets to his feet and with a bat traces in the infield the figure of a woman: head and hair, arms, legs, breasts, nipples. When he finishes, he whips out a knife and digs a little hole between the woman's opened legs.

"Huh? You know?"

I nod, and look away, across the outfield at the line of sycamores beyond right field, and then beyond that, across Heberton Street, where the houses are so big they rise above the tree line.

"Show me how it's done," Poe says.

I turn and look at him and know that I don't know him.

"You said you knew what to do. Show me what to do."

I think about running, but then I remember the cardinal rule of East Liberty: No matter what, pretend you don't care. Shut up and laugh. Even if you're dying.

"Go ahead. She won't mind."

The others continue to look at me.

"Maybe she's not your type," Poe says, unbuckling his belt.

He lets his pants drop and pulls down his underwear. Then he falls on the woman in the dirt and, for a few seconds, writhes between her legs, jumps up and yelps. Everyone laughs.

"You want a piece of that?" he says to me. "No? Who wants a piece of Francene Renzo?"

I glance off at the sycamores again. The highest branches are still winter-barkless, milky, like undressed flesh, bits of sun nailed to the white wood sluicing through the tree's inflorescence. Further down, the brown bark warps, the trunk gigantic, smoky.

My very favorite painting of Mickey's was a sycamore, so hauntingly real the way the shadows and light played off it, the heft of its scarred trunk, the abandon of its stripped creamy limbs. He called it "Sebastian," after the Byzantine iconographs displayed in our Missal of the breechclouted, bleeding martyr massacred by arrows in Rome. But he left out Sebastian. Just arrows stabbing out of the naked tree.

The others guys line up at the dirt effigy of Francene Renzo. But it doesn't matter. I'll never let on. I am a tree. A sycamore shot full of arrows.

• • •

The evening of the day after Mickey's funeral, Francene stands in her slip at the ironing board, ironing her dress for work the next day. Playing on the hi-fi is *West Side Story*. The song, "Somewhere." Francene singing along. She has a husky voice, but when she sings it is soft, soprano. I like her singing. Singing myself, under my breath, and thinking of Mickey, I bounce a tennis ball off the living room wall, which I know I'm not supposed to do.

"Stop playing with the ball," she snaps.

I always listen to her, but this time I keep it up.

"Bobby. What did I say?"

I start singing loudly, "Hold my hand and I'll take you there," drowning out the record. Then "somehow, someday, somewhere," over and over, "somehow, someday, somewhere," braying, and double-timing the ball off the wall till it gets away from me and bangs into the hi-fi. The stylus lurches and the needle screeches across the record.

She turns off the player, walks into the living room, and we lock up. We haven't wrestled in a long time and I am surprised at how much stronger I've grown. But I can't take her down. I fix her in a headlock, and she picks me up over her head and body-slams me onto the living room carpet, something she has never done before. I lay there on my back with the wind knocked out of me, staring at the chandelier vibrating from the ceiling. Mr. Gigante, our widower landlord who lives on the first floor, beats on his ceiling with a broom handle and shouts.

Francene circles, then swoops in and pancakes me so I can't budge. She gets me in the sleeper, one of the occult studio wrestling holds, her fingers digging deeper and deeper into the cavern where the trapezoid meets the carotid artery. I grow drowsy. In my back, through the floor, I feel the tip of Mr. Gigante's broomstick, vaguely hear his Piedmontese harangue.

Sleep darkens my shirt like sweat. It hasn't occurred to me to cry out, but when I do Francene falls off me. She looks so tired, so suddenly frail in that black slip. I notice it

is threadbare along the bodice. Rising up, I lift her in a
bearhug and drive her against a wall. A framed photograph
of Pope John the XXIII thuds down and the glass cracks
across his smiling, chubby face. Horrified, I instantly relent.

"Are you all right?" I ask.

"Yes," she says, very composed, backing away from me
into her bedroom, telling me good night as she closes the
door.

• • •

Finished with the woman in the infield, they start
toward the bikes.

"Let me ride your bike back," Poe says.

"Sure."

The cracked black bat leans aginst my bike. Poe picks
it up and bashes it off a tree until it shatters, then breaks in
half. I don't have a chance to even open my mouth.
Grinning, with his sunglasses on again, he holds the
splintered handle for a moment in his hand, then throws it
like a knife into the outfield, mounts my bike and speeds
off. I look down at what is left of the barrel, the white
trademark, still intact, face up. For a moment I contemplate
retrieving the pieces, but instead get on Poe's rusted,
fenderless bike and pedal after the others, back the way I
came, along the heavenly perfection of upper Stanton
Avenue, until I am back in East Liberty.

They sit on the steps, passing cigarettes, in one of Dilworth schoolyard's deep stairwells. Smoke rises out of it. The bikes line kickstanded on the slippery red cobblestones, mine on its side, its front wheel still almost imperceptibly spinning. Three of its spokes angle out from the bent rim and the tire is flat. None of them have looked up since I rode in.

I think of Hugo Zitelli, how I haven't seen him in so long, how Mrs. Zitelli never mentions him anymore. Francene says she heard he dropped out of the seminary and is selling shoes in Erie, that he has gone to pot. What a shame, Francene goes on to say.

There are people in the neighborhood who think being a priest is a cop-out, something boys do when they can't do anything else, not even join the service. And to top it off, Hugo won't even end up a priest, but instead spends all day tying and untying strangers' shoes. That's what Mrs. Zitelli gets for bragging, people say. But, really, she was a good mother. Doing for her and her son with no husband. No one deserves such misery and, in truth, Hugo, even if he is a little funny, is a good boy. But no gumption. And no father. On and on.

It has always confused me: to the onlooker, a person's misfortune—like Hugo's and Mrs. Zitelli's—can be both a shame and a source of satisfaction. But this is vintage East Liberty, where a smack in the head waits around every corner. Feeling sorry for someone is as close as anybody gets to feeling superior, and the next logical leap is contempt. Myself, I always liked Hugo; and I loved that music he used to play on those torrid summer nights when I couldn't sleep. But I always felt sorry for him, too.

On a weekend home from the seminary, he was cornered by the Jets and tied to the schoolyard fence facing Saint Marie Street. They pulled his trousers and underwear down to his ankles and left him. Much too old to cry, still wearing his tie and white shirt, his crotch as hairy as a man's, he cried and cried until his mother, wielding a butcher knife, cut him down, then followed the Jets down to the corner where they hung in front of Chookie's drinking wine and rolling craps.

She charged Fusco and tried to stick him, but he danced out of the way and the rest of them taunted her until she fell apart and said she was going to kill herself right there with her own knife, and the Jets said they would like that. Mrs. Pezzulo called the cops who came and carted Mrs. Zitelli off as the Jets scattered. Poor Hugo, poor Mrs. Zitelli, I want to say; but in East Liberty, that's like saying the hell with them, they got what they deserved.

Francene says she doesn't think Hugo ever went to the seminary, that Mrs. Zitelli made it all up, like her dead husband for whom she's disguised herself in black all these years. Francene is probably right. Probably to Mrs. Zitelli, an imaginary priest for a son is infinitely better than a flesh-and-blood shoe salesman, or whatever. Now all Mrs. Zitelli does is pour salt on the slugs around her garbage cans and sit on her porch with a rosary.

Francene says Hugo will never come back again. She tells me about the duck, Alfred, how cute it and Hugo were, how he was so mad about it. They kept it in a box in the kitchen where all it did was eat duck mash and go to the bathroom. Mrs. Zitelli tolerated it because Hugo adored it and she expected it would die soon. But it thrived, and every few weeks it had to be shifted to a bigger box that would be sodden within the hour, and the kitchen stinking. Mrs. Zitelli, a zealot when it came to cleanliness, grew to hate the duck. She found it worrisome and particularly disgraceful that her nearly grown boy who had hair sprouting prematurely on his face should have such a filthy pet.

Once the duck was full-grown, Hugo built a chicken wire pen for it in the backyard, but it learned to squeeze its head through the wire and bite the heads off Mrs. Zitelli's zinnias. It squawked all night. It became an adult duck and showed no signs of dying. Mrs. Zitelli suggested donating it to the zoo, but Hugo wouldn't hear of it. He trained Alfred to follow him up and down Collins Avenue. The whole neighborhood marveled at this, but the duck accentuated Hugo's oddness and gave them more license to make fun of him. A father would not permit his son to walk a duck like a dog.

Two Easters after Mrs. Zitelli brought home the tiny duckling for her son, she decided at dawn to slaughter it for Easter dinner while Hugo was at the church helping Father Vita pull the purple shrouds off the statues for the gladdest morning of the Church calendar. She crept into the backyard with her butcher knife, and unfastened the pen's gate. The Resurrection sun was just rolling pinkly down the alley. Alfred, who despised Mrs. Zitelli, turned and nipped at her, then squawked. She spoke lovingly to him. "Come, Mr. *Anatra*. Mr. Duck. Let me give you a little kiss with this blade." But he spread his wings and lunged with his sharp beak. She couldn't get near him.

She fetched a long handled garden spade and hammered at him until he was so woozy he fell over. Then she fell on him with the knife and hacked his head off. By the time she was ready to leave for church in her best black dress, Alfred was dressed and in the refrigerator.

Francene can't help laughing as she tells the story.

"I don't believe it," I say, sort of laughing myself.

"Well, I'm afraid it's true."

"So what happened?"

When Hugo and Mrs. Zitelli arrived home from Mass together, she popped Alfred in the oven, and the next time Hugo saw his pet, masquerading as a large chicken, was on the Easter table next to the manicotti and rice cakes. The meat was extremely tough and bruised from the shovel. But the real joke is that Mrs. Zitelli was unaware that a duck over six months, much less one that is two years old, is practically inedible. The flesh is like leather.

Francene is laughing again.

"What did Hugo do when he found out?" I ask.

"I don't know. Poor kid."

"Poor kid? Why are you laughing then?"

"I can't help it. Why are you?"

● ● ●

I jump off Poe's bike, roll it over to the stairwell and stand there until they finally look up at me. Poe, lounging at the very bottom, smiles. In one motion I try to military press the bike and heave it down on top of Poe, but it is too heavy. It bumps straight down the stairs on its tires until the handlebars twist. Then it skids the rest of the way on its side, sparking and banging to the bottom, clipping several of them scrambling to get out of the way.

Poe shoots up to the top of the stairs and gets as close to me as he can without touching, my forehead even with his chin. I can't see his eyes behind the sunglasses, but he smiles again, the broken tooth somehow humanizing him. We have done a lot of things together; we are friends. I smile back. He shifts a touch to his right like a second baseman beginning his pivot on a double play and I am suddenly blinded by the sun. Then he sucker-punches me just like Francene did after the National Record Mart.

But this fist has in it the kind of hurt men visit on one another. An intimation of death. Like walking into an invisible wall. Nothing to prepare you for the shock, the fright and stupor it throws you in. I am Poe's sucker, the kind W. C. Fields said never to give an "even break."

Surprised to still be on my feet, I bring my hand up to my jaw. I do not feel so much injured as astonished. Poe no longer smiles. I charge him, but he knocks me down with another punch; and when I get up he bowls me over and pounds me unmercifully with his fists. I want to fight, but I can't move, my entire body numb.

Poe steps over to my bike and kicks out the spokes on the rear wheel. I try again to push off the cobblestones, but my arms are mush. In my life I have never cried in front of anyone but Francene. I feel all of them ringing me, waiting for me to flinch so they can kill me. Rolling myself into a ball, I cradle my head with my arms, and clamp my eyes as I fight to not make the slightest sound, to not even breathe until they have all gone away. Someone throws a lit cigarette down on me. There is laughter, the clinking of bicycle chains chewed by flywheels. The smell of my smoldering dungarees.

Walking Hugo's disabled bike back home, I find myself thinking about Confirmation. It is only about a month away. I envision the ancient, palsied Bishop singling me out and asking me to recite the "Memorare," which I know by heart from hours of study. I stand. The church is packed. The assembled congregation regards me. Francene wears a big, red-banded hat with a snap brim and peacock feather. I can see her only from the nose down, but she is smiling, her red lips slightly parted to reveal the tips of her teeth.

I am suddenly afflicted with amnesia. I not only can't remember the "Memorare," but I can't remember anything. I am void. The Bishop drags his half-paralyzed body down off the altar to where I sit with the other candidates. He lifts his staff. A tiny bubble of spit breaks on his upper lip. His nostrils are cavernous. I break into an uncontrollable fit of laughter, and continue howling even after he clobbers me again and again with his stick.

I don't know. It's the pain, I guess. Poe beat the living hell out of me. I hurt all over. And then the bat, and my bike. I don't know what to do. I don't even have a sponsor for Confirmation. I know three guys, Uncle John, Nonno and my father. The first two are dead and my father's a figment. Francene always says complaining is for losers, so I guess I need to shut up and play my hand. Something will work out.

One of the poker players at Nardini's, a hunchback guy they called Creature, went home broke every day. When he came out of the back room, busted, he'd look at Mickey and me over at the pool tables, throw up his hands, like what the heck, wink and say, "Maybe I'll hit a number."

EAST LIBERTY

CHAPTER 11

Parked in front of our house is an immaculate, tangerine Cadillac convertible, top down, with cream interior. Mr. Gigante sits on the front porch with a long, smelly cigar launched under his bristly little mustache. He wears plaid pants and bedroom slippers, a V-necked white T-shirt, his neck spangled with a gold chain, cross, and the Italian good luck horn to ward off the eyes. He's bald on top, but his hair along the sides whips back, resembling fins.

With him is his dog, Baby, a Chinese pug who favors Edward G. Robinson. Baby is disgusting. He slobbers and grunts. At bedtime, his chainsaw-like snores travel up the ductwork and broadcast through our vents, so that on certain nights we cannot get to sleep. Mr. Gigante allows him to go to the bathroom in the apartment's communal backyard. Francene has to juke around small piles of shit when she hangs clothes to dry.

When Mr. Gigante sees me, he says, "What the hell happened to you, huh?"

I'm tempted to tell him, but I say, "Nothing."

"Nothing, huh? You should see the other guy, huh?"

Baby, thrumming like an idling engine, plants his back paws and scoots side to side on his front paws, occasionally lunging and kissing Mr. Gigante on the mouth. His short tail loops back on itself into a perfect O.

Francene and I make fun of Mr. Gigante all the time. The way he dresses. Those plaid and checked pants he keeps hiked almost to his armpits, that most of his body resides beneath his beltline. The way his eyes bulge out of the sockets each time he hits his cigar. He ends each sentence with "huh?" and still fancies himself a lady's man. In fact, he keeps at least one of those goo-goo, cigar-stogie eyes on Francene at all times.

Sometimes to give Francene a charge, I waltz out of my bedroom wearing a V-neck T-shirt, ropes of her chains around my neck, a pretzel stick for a cigar, my pants pulled way up. I comb my hair back on the sides and hunch over. I say: "Hey Francene, huh? You wanna go up to the Sons of Columbus, huh? To my lodge and have dinner with me, huh? Me and you, huh? You look good, huh? You know, huh? Huh? Huh?"

Francene falls apart laughing, then grunts like Baby.

Mr. Gigante says, "You see that Cadillac, huh? The owner of that boat is upstairs in your apartment, huh?"

He and Baby kiss.

I want to tell him, "We make fun of you all the time," but then I have this peculiar feeling that the man upstairs with Francene is my father.

I leave my bike on the sidewalk, take the stairs two at a time to our apartment, walk in the front door and slowly down the hall toward the kitchen. A man sits at the kitchen table with his back to me. A blue suitcoat, with faint white stripes, drapes off the back of his chair. He is so broad that the chair looks like a board attached to his white-shirted back. The hair on the back of his head is oily and corrugated, and he drinks something rusty from a juice glass.

When he turns I see that he is not my father. He is too old, and looks nothing like the man who killed the bat. It occurs to me for the first time in my life that I have never seen a photograph of my father.

"How you doing?" he says. "You must be Bobby."

"Yeah."

He stands and swings at me an immense, outstretched hand and we shake. His face is beat up, rubbery, pocked; and his smile is so big and wide it's like a hinge cracking his whole face in half. From his belt up he's huge, his starched white shirt packed with muscle, no neck, and he's sweating. For a second I think he's Bruno Samartino, but he's too old to be Bruno.

"I'm Carl," he says, sitting back down. Then, just like Mr. Gigante, "What happened to you?"

"I was playing ball."

"Oh, okay, I see. C'mere."

I walk closer to him. There is a horizontal divot at the bridge of his nose.

"Make a fist," he says.

I make a fist, tucking my thumb inside my fingers.

"Not like that. Like this."

He holds up a fist the size of a softball, a signet ring on the ring finger and what looks like a diamond on the pinky, the thumb knotted over the four closed fingers. He points at my fist. "You hit a guy like that and you'll break your thumb. Let me show you something else. Say you're fighting a guy. If you can, bust him in the nose. And just as you're landing, twist your fist."

In slow motion, he throws his fist against my nose and snaps it counterclockwise on contact. "Guaranteed to break a guy's nose and produce a ton of blood. Most guys'll quit right there. But not me. Look at this nose."

He turns sideways so I can get a better view of his mangled nose, then holds up seven fingers. "Been broken seven times." He takes a handkerchief out of his back pocket, unfolds it, then wipes the sweat from his face and neck.

"I boxed professionally for several years. I fought Fritzie Zivic and Billy Conn. Lost both fights in decisions, and gave them each hell. You know, you should be more careful when you're playing ball."

I would like to laugh at his joke. I know it's the polite thing to do. And it's not even that I don't like Carl. I just want him out of our house.

"I've known women to take a long time getting ready," Carl says, "but your mother takes the cake."

"Get out of here," I say.

He studies me with his entire, battered, bemused face. He thinks I'm kidding at first, but after a moment he says, "What are you talking about?"

"I want you to leave our house."

"What are you talking about, kid? What's the matter with you?"

"I just want you to get out of here right now."

"Who the hell do you think you're talking to, you fresh punk? I could break you in half," Carl says, looming over me.

Perfectly willing to be broken in half, I remain silent, staring into Carl's quizzical, not quite angry, face until another kind of a look comes over it—a beaten-down relief, pitiful, really—and he snatches his suitcoat and lumbers out of the house. I pour myself a glass of milk and sit down at the table to wait for Francene.

● ● ●

I don't know the year, but it is summer, late, late Friday night, actually early Saturday morning, and we are living on Lincoln Avenue. Francene and I have just finished

watching *Spellbound*. I love Alfred Hitchcock movies, but
they invariably give me the creeps, though I don't admit
this to Francene. As soon as we switch the set off, the vague
racket we have been hearing all night from upstairs in
Cooney and Hattie's apartment grows instantly louder.

For the first two or three hours of his unpredictable
drunks, Cooney is happy. He sings old Irish songs and jigs
Hattie around their apartment, shaking the pipes and
ductwork in the whole duplex. Then he gets maudlin and
cries about his old mother he had to leave back in Ireland
and how, God willing, they'll be reunited in Heaven. This
gives way to tirades against the mayor, Whiskey Joe Barr
himself, and the whole lot of corrupt, on-the-take Pittsburgh
politicians, how they drummed good men like him off the
police force with half the pension he was owed and now
the city is run by hunkies and wops and niggers. From below,
Francene and I chart his progress.

"Where is he now, Bobby?" Francene asks.

"Imagining a sup of tea from the hob of his mother's
fine, golden house in heaven."

She laughs. "Is he crying yet?"

"Uh uh."

"Let me know when he gets to the hunkies, wops and
niggers."

It is usually at that point that his fifth of rye will nudge
him in one of two directions. Cooney will pass out—we

frequently hear and feel the telltale thud—or he'll go for his pistol.

Tonight he turns on Hattie. She's a sow-whore and a chippie, nothing more than pigshit Irish. He'd rather eat what's mucked from a sty than the swill she serves him.

Hattie is long-suffering. She says things like, "Now, Cooney, you don't really mean that." And "You'll make yourself sick going on like this." She reminds me of Susan Hayward in *Snows of Kilimanjaro* who takes all that drunken guff from Gregory Peck, though Hattie is much, much older than Hayward. It makes Francene furious.

"I'd give him 'You'll make yourself sick.' The minute he passed out, I'd pulverize him with the iron."

"Get out," Cooney is screaming. "You get your goddam rags and leave my house, you streetwalking, straphanging slut."

We hear slamming and stomping, then the clop of Cooney descending the stairs, the door slamming and his tripping around on the front porch.

"Oh, oh," says Francene, "He's out on the porch."

But then we hear the door again and Cooney pounding back up the stairs. After a few rounds of this, there's a knock on the door. Hattie wants Francene to come up and try to calm him down.

"He's got half a package on him now, Fran," she says. "He says I have to leave. He's throwing all my clothes in the front yard. Jesus." She wears an apron over her housecoat, smokes a cigarette and tries to smile.

"I'll be right up," Francene assures her.

We look out our living room window and see clothes strewn across the yard and sidewalk. I'm afraid to stay in the apartment alone, so Francene takes me with her.

Hattie sits at the kitchen table and cries while Cooney stuffs her clothes through the kitchen window.

"I told him," she says tearily, "in your condition you shouldn't be traipsing up and down the steps. You're liable to fall. So . . . "

She gestures toward Cooney who turns to us. Behind him, through the open window, a white and flimsy bit of clothing blows off.

"Well, look who's here," he says. "Mother Courage, herself, and her wee stripling."

"Good evening, Cooney," says Francene. "We were enjoying the performance so much through the ceiling, we decided to come up and witness it in person."

Cooney takes a protracted gander at Francene. Like a gambler deciding whether to see a lavish bet or fold. Barefooted, his toenails marbled yellow, he wears a heavy herringbone suit with a ratty white T-shirt under it. His forearms are like Popeye's. I sidle closer to Francene and look around for something I can bash him with if he charges. That gun is around somewhere.

"Why don't we have some coffee," Francene suggests.

"Capital idea," says Cooney, his big, spud face suddenly cragged with a grin.

"I'll hurry and make some," says Hattie.

"Do that, you old battle-ax, while I and my emerald-eyed beauty take a turn over the linoleum."

With great pomp he bows and holds out his hand. Francene takes it and they spin about the kitchen. Cooney is actually quite graceful as he dances, looking straight into Francene's eyes, smiling that thick-lipped smile. When they finish, he kisses her hand and collapses into one of the chairs, breathing heavily and sweating.

"Thank you, dear lady, thank you," he gasps. "Now you must consent to being my sweetheart."

"That's a tempting offer, Cooney. But Hattie is your sweetheart."

"Hattie is in love with Perry Como, that failed wop barber from Canonsburg. She has never cared a thing for me."

"You know that's not true, dear," trills Hattie. "I just like the way he sings. Why don't you let me tuck you in now?"

"You may tuck your she-serpent's tongue in your gob, slattern." He bangs his fist on the table.

"Let's have our coffee," Hattie says in a tiny, trembling voice.

"To the blackest corner of hell with you and your coffee, woman. Where's my whiskey?"

Francene stands directly is front of where he sits. "You are not being much of a gentleman, Cooney. I think you should apologize to Hattie."

"Not until I have another dram of rye and teach the stripling here how it is a man handles a gun." And with that he pulls a pistol out from beneath his coat. Like the gun in *Spellbound*, it appears gigantic, like another living thing has entered the room, that of its own volition it will blow the whole house apart.

Cooney's thick finger is on the trigger. He is going to kill us. That's all there is to it and I can't remember a single prayer, nor can I move even though Hattie is crying and saying, "Please, Cooney," over and over and Francene holds out her arms and calls me to her.

"Come here, stripling," says Cooney.

He is smiling again.

"I just want to teach him."

He holds out toward me his flat palm with the gun lying in it. Francene takes the bottle from the sink and pours a waterglass full.

"Take the gun, lad," he says very gently, smiling.

I unroot myself and take a step.

Bobby," Francene says, her voice just on the edge of extreme.

"Nobody move," Cooney says. "I have killed men with this hardhearted friend of mine."

Hattie falls into a chair, lays her head in her arms and sobs.

My feet take me not to Francene, but toward the gun.

"Take it," says Cooney.

Francene moves between us and sets the whiskey on the table. "Apologize to Hattie, give me the gun and go to bed," she says.

Cooney looks at the glass, then at Francene and smiles. He picks it up and I see his cracked teeth through the underside of the glass as he drains half of it. His body convulses, then slackens.

"For a kiss from the winsome Francene Renzo I will obey."

"Apologize first."

"I am so sorry, blossom," he says, smiling, to the top of Hattie's shuddering head on the table.

"Now the gun."

He stands shakily and hands Francene the gun. Then he finishes off in a gulp what's left in the glass. Again there is a declension in his bearing, as if his bones are slowly dissolving and any second he will go down. But he summons enough strength to seize Francene, pinning her arms to her body and squeezing until, arched backwards, she drops the gun. Then he grinds his wet, stubbly mouth against hers as

I conjure an image of his annihilation and sear him with my eyes. My eyes, the same shape-shifting green of Francene's. Eyes like the *gatto*, the cat, Nonna claims.

Francene finally works her arms up to his chest and shoves him off. He staggers and steadies himself on a chairback. She wipes her mouth with the back of one hand, then the other.

"Are you sure you would not like the full measure of my charms?" he asks, going down in the chair.

"I'll pass. Thanks anyway."

Cooney smiles, wags a finger, begins to say something, but before he can, he and the chair capsize and he is stone cold, his cheek against the floor.

Hattie jumps to her feet and the three of us stare at him for a moment.

"He'll be quiet now," Hattie says. "You may kick him if you want, Fran. He'll never know. I do it myself sometimes."

"Maybe some other time. I don't know how you put up with this, Hattie."

"It's not so bad, Fran. You have to understand that I love him, and he loves me."

"He has a funny way of showing it."

"Well, dear, we all have, really. Help me get him into the bedroom, then I can manage after that."

They each take a foot and drag Cooney out of the kitchen and down the long linoleumed hall to the bedroom.

176

I pick up the gun. In my hand it is heavy, inert, cold and black. Gently I set it on the table, wash my hands in the sink and have a cup of coffee.

When Hattie and Francene return, Francene picks up the gun, runs water in a saucepan on the counter and drops it in. Her mouth is bleeding, but then I see that it's just her lipstick smeared.

"Let's go, Bobby."

Hattie and Francene hug.

"I'm sorry, Fran, I don't know what I'd do without you."

"Don't you worry about it. Try and get a little sleep before Prince Charming wakes up."

"I'll have a big breakfast waiting for him."

"Don't forget the ground glass," Francene says.

Hattie bends and kisses me. "Don't think the worst of Cooney, Bobby."

"I won't," I lie, having already made my peace with him.

• • •

Francene says she's feeling a little wound up and wants to take the air. Who the heck could sleep after Cooney, anyhow, and besides it's twenty after five in the morning.

We sit on the concrete blocks that wall our front yard from the sidewalk. Light fans out behind us, glancing off the windows of the empty 82 Lincoln sliding slowly along the trolley rails sunk in cobblestone. The avenue is deserted, yet we can make out music and a few cries, like birds passing far off, a quarter of a mile away down on Frankstown Avenue with its black speakeasies and honky-tonks.

"Live it up," Francene whispers.

"Huh, Francene?"

"Nothing."

Sirens whooping, an ambulance flies across Lincoln at Meadow. Behind it crawl three of Stagno's big bread trucks delivering bread to stores and other bakeries. The sun crowns and banks left into the branches of our mulberry tree. Its fruit is so ripe and wet with dew it drips prisms of sunlight into Francene's long hair. I lean over and lay my head in her lap. She lights a cigarette, traces my eyebrows with her finger, then down my nose and along my lips.

"I'm sorry," she says, but I suppose I'm already asleep.

The high, blue-skied knell of Our Lady of the Help of Christians' church bells wakes me. The sun has stolen out of the mulberry tree and balances on Francene's shoulder. Next to me on the blanket upon which I'm curled, she pares with purple hands peaches with a steak-knife, slicing them into a bowl already filled with mulberries. There are two bowls of vanilla ice cream, a thermos of coffee and two cups.

"I thought we'd have breakfast out here," she says, wiping her hands on a tea towel. "Hungry?"

Half-blinded by the dazzle, I work my way to a sitting

position. The old, stooped Italian people in their Sunday raiment work their ways along the sidewalk to nine o'clock Mass at Our Lady's, the service said every Sunday in Italian by old Father D'Avia, the priest who baptized not only me, but Francene as well. They stare at us, eating ice cream and fruit in our front yard. Francene smiles at them as they pass, and says *Buongiorno* or *Como esta*. They seem to like this and smile back, the sun catching the gold in their teeth. *Bene, Ciao,* they answer. With great formality, the men tip their hats.

I'm pretty sure I'm awake, but what I see next makes me think I'm dreaming. It's a silver Corvette, *the* silver Corvette, from the TV show, *Route 66*, cruising slowly out of the sun along Lincoln from Frankstown. At the wheel is George Maharis and, riding shotgun, Martin Milner. Maybe Cooney gunned us down and we're marooned in some fantastic limbus until God decides what to do with us. Either that, or it's a miracle.

Francene is on her feet, both hands visoring her eyes against the sun that has fallen from her shoulder and bounced along Lincoln where it now sits like the Second Coming on the trunk of the Corvette.

Even movie stars cannot fail to notice her. Maharis and Milner wave, but she is too blinded to trust this vision, so she remains transfixed and motionless until I tug on the hem of her pink dress and she sits back down, dumbstruck.

For the next seven days, unlikely as it is, an episode of

Route 66 is shot in and outside of a Negro mortuary directly across the street from our house. Two tractor-trailers and various other vehicles camp along two blocks of Lincoln. Sixteen hours a day, dozens of men and women pour in and out of them. Taxis come and go. In addition to Maharis and Milner, the show's hip stars, it features the legendary Ethel Waters, and Lee Aaker who played Rusty in *Rin Tin Tin*.

I never really catch the plot. Most of the filming takes place indoors. All I know is that Ethel Waters is an old, dying Blues singer who wants to get together one last time with her old band, and Maharis and Milner set out in the Corvette to round them up. I watch take after take as men and women, dressed in black and crying, come out of the mortuary behind a casket borne by six black pallbearers, before the director, a tiny man with a purple baseball cap and a headset over it, says they have it right. I've sat on the porch and witnessed this very thing take place so many times in actuality, I cannot quite make the distinction between real life and acting.

The silver Corvette remains parked at the curb in front of the big, black stone fortress. Occasionally Maharis and Milner bolt out of the mortuary, vault into the car without opening its doors, and lay tire for half a block in the eye of the camera. Then they inch back to their space in reverse and go back inside. Every day after lunch the stars come out to the sidewalk, which has been roped off by the police, and sign autographs for the throngs of people camped there.

Francene hustles home every day during her lunch hour for autographs. I watch her talking to Maharis, how they smile and nod at each other. He takes off his sunglasses and hands them to her. She puts them on with great flair and poses. They both laugh. When she takes them off to give them back, he tells her to keep them.

Every night we have supper on our front porch and watch them shoot until dark. One night Maharis joins us. Ham-and-egg sandwiches, Isaly's potato salad, nonpareils and red pistachios. Francene goes in and brings back candles for the table. Her dress is the same color as her eyes. It has white polka dots with gold trim and shiny, gold, plasticky pagodas floating among the polka dots. As it gets darker and darker, the pagodas glow in the dark. Maharis lights her cigarettes.

Francene's teeth glow in the dark, too, on top of the terraces of pagodas and the parabola of her cigarette as she moves it from her mouth to the ashtray. His high cheek bones glint like mirrors. His hair is trained. Shirt sleeves rolled up to the middle of his biceps. He says he loved the meal. Thanks. Do I like ice cream? Do I want to sit in the Corvette? Parked tonight on our side of the street.

There's enough light even in the dark for me to see the red leather interior and the controls on the cockpit dash. I open the door and climb in on the passenger side.

"No," he says.

Behind the wheel, he meant. I figure he's kidding.

"No," he says again. "I mean it. Get behind the wheel."

So I slide over and take the wheel, let my right hand fall to the stick and close my eyes.

Francene says she wishes she had a camera. But it's too dark.

"Tomorrow," Maharis says, "I'll get one of the guys to take a picture. Let's go for a ride tonight. Let's get some ice cream."

"You never answered me about the ice cream," he says to me. "You like ice cream, don't you?"

I tell him I do.

"Hop in the back," he says.

I dive over the seat. He helps Francene in, then whirls around the car and slips into the cockpit and turns the key. The car spasms to life with a rhythmic, predatory power.

When he hits the throttle we lurch an entire block, the engine percolating like it might explode if Maharis doesn't floor it. And then he does and we lift off the ground, his arms in the darting shimmer of streetlights corded on the steering wheel and I am scared the way I was on the Jackrabbit at Kennywood, but not that I will die. Thrilled scared without the danger, and feeling immortal in the back of the silver Corvette convertible tooling up North Lincoln past Joe Westray's Ebony Lounge where the street and sidewalk in front of the club swell with revelling black men with processes drinking spodi-odi out of paper sacks and exotic brown women with red jewelry and red hair, the music from inside banging out the door into the dark, hot summer night.

They all stare, then turn as we blow by. A garish hot pink moon sits on the steeple of Corpus Christi Church. Francene and I make the Sign of the Cross as we pass. But Maharis doesn't. She has told me he is Greek and they have their own religion. George, she calls him.

At the Dairy Queen next to Silver Lake Drive-in, carved into a hill under the Larimer Bridge, on Washington Boulevard, we get ice cream cones and sit in the lot eating them as the giant, silent figures from the distant movie screen loom up in the darkness: Jackie Gleason and Paul Newman, veiled in cigarette smoke and wielding pool cues, leer at each other across a pool table, then shoot. Unbelievable strokes, the balls finding the pockets across the green felt as though magnetized.

"Only in the movies," Francene says, the smoke from her cigarette spiraling up to mingle with the smoke on the screen. Above us, the bridge is invisible in the blackness, but the cars make a whispering noise as they cross.

"Where's the lake?" George asks.

Francene and I laugh.

"There's no lake," she says.

• • •

Every night, Francene and George take a drive in the Corvette. I watch them like I'm watching a movie: the way he holds the door for her and helps her in, how he leaps behind the wheel, then the car sizzling away from the curb and Francene's hair flowing out behind her.

They sit in the Corvette at the curb in front of our house and talk. She lays her hand on his wrist. He untangles a strand of hair from her lips. Finally they kiss. Then they talk some more. Perhaps they say to each other, "I love you." Perhaps they will marry and George will be my father. I wonder what my life will be like in Hollywood.

On the morning of the last day of shooting, George walks across Lincoln to where Francene and I sit in the yard. He asks her if she wants to be in the episode. She looks at him like, "You're kidding." But he's not kidding. Nothing big, he tells her. No speaking. Probably no Academy Award, he laughs.

"No, that's okay," she says. "I mean, yes, I'd love to."

This is it. What we've both been waiting for. Francene rushes into the house to get dolled up.

It's Sunday so all of East Liberty is gathered on the set. A thousand people, I'd bet, and all of them see a white limousine pull up to the curb in front of the mortuary, the driver jumping out of his seat and racing to open the passenger door for Francene Renzo, who for all the world looks like Jackie Kennedy. So polished, they need only two takes. But I could watch it all day. The chauffeur's black hand on the back door. First a leg and the black high heel, then Francene with dark glasses and a wide-brimmed feathery hat with a veil, one hand holding it in place as she emerges from the car in a black dress, a string of pearls, the face steely, betraying nothing, but in it a childlike reflex toward sorrow. Without looking left or right, she clips up the walk into the mortuary and disappears.

The next morning, very early, George comes over to say good-bye. Francene stands out on the porch with him for a long time, then has to run down the street to the carstop because she's late for work. Across the street they carry that coffin out of the mortuary one more time and then they're gone. Up the ramps into the trucks, headed west, way west, the silver Corvette lashed to its own trailer and towed. The sky is the color of concrete. I go back to bed.

When I wake it is raining, and I am sopping wet. Burning wet. I realize I have peed the bed, and am choked with panic because more than anything I'm sure I'm dying. I strip the bed, change it, then wad the soiled sheets into a grocery bag, and take them outside to dump in our trash drum.

For breakfast I have graham crackers and milk. Out of the concrete sky, the rain pelts down. I begin reading *Treasure Island*, but have to stop when Billy Bones dies after the "black spot" is delivered to him. I stash the book under the couch and turn on every light in the house. I'm old enough to stay home alone during the summer; Hattie looks in on me every so often. "Have you eaten, Bobby?" she'll say. "I can fix you a tuna sandwich with watercress." I hate tuna fish, and I don't know what watercress is. She tells me if I get lonesome to come up with her and Cooney, but Cooney, in a T-shirt and pajama bottoms, is working through his tea to his whiskey. He holds his pistol and he is twice as dangerous with an audience.

Francene has left lunch. A can of tomato soup and wrapped in wax paper six saltines with lids, peanut butter and jelly in the middle, a peach and two peanut clusters.

During the day I never turn on television because it spooks me. Videotaped shows like *Secret Storm*, and commercials for Tide and Lucky Strike. I get the feeling that I'm the only one watching, that everyone else is gone. Outside the curtain of gray rain seals off the world. No people. No traffic. I don't even like the looks of the television set, its stolid, ugly clairvoyance. I keep thinking it'll click on by itself and something will crawl out of it. After days of *Route* 66 across the street, everything is preternaturally quiet.

CHAPTER 12

Clamping on my Pirates cap, I walk into the rain and take the mound. I'm pitching with only two lousy days' rest, and my arm is hanging. I wear long sleeves so no one can see how swollen and black and blue my elbow is. The rain doesn't help. It chills my arm and each time I let go of the ball, electricity jolts through the elbow and my fingers go numb. No one throws in the bullpen. Like a gargoyle, Murtaugh perches on the top step of the dugout, wearing a hardhat to keep his head dry, his jaw swamped with tobacco. Mantle, batting left-handed and drenched in his coarse gray away-flannels with NEW YORK across the breast, stands in the muddy box.

The faces in the stands, beneath the umbrellas and the rain, melt together. Strangers waiting at the edge for things to end. Ed Vargo, calling balls and strikes, straightens, raises both hands and shouts so that the entire infield and both dugouts can hear him. "We're going on with this no matter what." Then he resumes his crouch behind Smoky.

The *Press* says I'm moody, that my reputation is undeserved and that I drink too much. I'm a goldbrick. I've been seen in the black clubs up in the Hill District, drunk as a lord, sitting in on jazz sets with Harold Betters on the trombone.

They printed that on our last trip to Frisco I started a fight in the Hilton lobby with a crippled guy. That's not true. The guy had a slight limp, and outweighed me by fifty pounds. He was drunk. Called me a guinea. I walked away.

They say the Pirates will deal me in the off-season, that I'm washed up, my marriage on the rocks. My kids are old enough to read the crap they write. I refuse to talk to the *Press*. If they knew about my arm, they'd dice me up for the buzzards. Because I mind my business, I've always been misunderstood.

I wonder if they'd like to face Mantle in the World Series with the score tied in front of an anxious, hometown thirty-five grand with nothing better to do than worry about my personal life.

I say the rosary between innings. I visit the poor kids in Children's Hospital, sign their casts, whatever. No matter what I'm asked to do, I smile and say no problem. Murtaugh—he can go to hell. Try playing for him some time. If I'm no good, then why am I out here facing Mantle with only two days' rest and an arm with a demon living in it. And the hell with this rain. Smoky wants a fastball, but

I figure in this weather Mantle's sitting on a fastball. I shake Smoky off and he goes through the whole ritual again: punches his mitt twice—that's the indicator, gives me a target, scoops up a handful of dirt and throws it down, then flashes the last three fingers of his right hand. Fastball.

No, Smoky. I shake him off again. He waddles out to the mound. Vargo paces behind the plate. He wants to get this game in. It's coming down in buckets, and the temperature has dropped fifteen degrees since the game started. My elbow feels like someone's turning a pipe wrench on it.

Smoky asks in his high-pitched, Southern way, "What the hell you shaking me off for?"

"He's waiting on a fastball," I tell him. "And he's not getting one. Not from me. I'm feeding him strictly offspeed and breaking balls."

"It's your funeral," Smoky says and turns his back on me.

"Get your fat carcass behind the plate and catch," I say to myself.

Thunder. I turn toward center and see the flag convulsing in the gale. Lightning stabs down over the 457 mark. Mantle looks bored, or tired. He knows my arm is shot and it's only a matter of time before the pain forces me into letting up. He knows all about pain. He invented pain. I wind up and throw the curve. When I snap it off, it hurts so badly I think

I've broken my arm, but I know it's a good pitch. It does that amazing, unexpected thing a perfect curve does, bending and dipping, like a whiplash in slow motion. Impossible to hit because you find yourself mesmerized, the way you might gape at a shooting star or an automobile out of control.

And that's what happens to Mantle. He's entranced by it until it's almost in Smoky's glove. Then he picks it out of the air like he's swiping your eyeteeth, and the ball rockets up and over the roof in right field. I don't know where it goes after that. It might still be travelling.

Over the roof, no less. No one but Babe Ruth has ever done that before. Smoky's vindicated. Vargo's disgusted. The crowd boos. Mantle trots the bases like an old horse in the rain. Like a little more wet, one way or another, doesn't mean a thing to him. He can go back to the clubhouse now and get his poor legs unwrapped.

Here comes Murtaugh with that sad, raccoon face. He doesn't say a word. I hand him the ball and head for the dugout. The crowd boos harder as I come off the field. I lift my cap. They throw things. The rain slaps me in the face.

• • •

Hattie yells out a window for me to get out of the rain. Can't I see that it's starting to lightning?

It's dark as night. The trees pitch, and lightning stitches the sky. I walk into the house, tug off my waterlogged clothes and sit naked on the lip of the tub. It's twenty minutes after six. Francene is usually home at six o'clock sharp. Something has happened. She's not coming home. She just pretended to go to work this morning; she's gone off to Hollywood with George.

I don't know what to do. Then I think to look through her closet. Her clothes are all there. In her dresser, I find among her things my birth certificate and savings bonds with my name on them. Maybe she didn't pack. Once out there she'll be able to afford everything new.

There is a big boom, then a flash. The light fizzes into blackness. In the war movies, the brave guys always confess that they were scared even as they performed the most fearless deeds. I'm scared, as scared as I've ever been. Beyond the window, the world is gray, even the grass; the sky is white, thunder rolling over everything and lightning veining out of it. I put on dry clothes and knock on Hattie and Cooney's door. As always, they are in the kitchen which is lit by a dozen votive candles.

"I was just coming down to look in on you, Bobby," Hattie says. She holds a spatula. From the gas range behind her drifts the smell of bacon and eggs frying. Cooney, barefoot, wearing a pajama shirt over his suit pants, sits at his customary spot at the table, his hand curled around a mug. In the candlelight he resembles Lon Chaney as the old, jaded lawman in *High Noon*.

191

"Have a set there, young Bob," he says, smiling. "Hattie, pour up a mug of tea for this fine fellow. And another for me too, would you, please?"

Cooney doctors my tea, like his, with milk and sugar. Hattie wears men's tennis shoes and hums as she cooks. Cooney tells me how he was a beat cop in Oakland in 1935 when Babe Ruth and the Boston Braves arrived at Forbes Field to play the Pirates. Ruth was at the end of his string and had a big red whiskey face, but he still put on a show of royalty.

It was hard Depression then and little shanty encampments had sprouted beyond the walls of the field. The Babe waltzed through them like the Pope himself, throwing from his big beaver coat dollar bills like confetti among the poor ragamuffins. Cooney had the pleasure of shaking his hand.

"And don't you know, that night he hit the last three home runs of his life, the last sailing clear over the right field roof, something no one else had ever done. I witnessed it myself. It turned into a white bird and flew and then it just disappeared," Cooney says, snapping his fingers. "Like that. Right here in this very town. Babe Ruth's last home run. Why, there's a gold plaque fastened to the right field wall at Forbes Field commemorating that very day. Have you ever seen William Bendix in *The Babe Ruth Story*, young Bob?"

"Yes," I say, remembering the solemn nuns showing it,

as if it were a parable, to all eight grades from a clattering sixteen-millimeter projector in the school basement.

"I cry every time I see it," Hattie says without turning her back from the stove.

"Hattie can't bear a maudlin story. She's too tenderhearted. I'm the only maudlin story she can suffer."

"I don't suffer you, Cooney. I put up with you."

"Well, it's a sad tale any way you slice it. Now they like to make much over what a rummy was the Babe and a great rounder and so forth, but he hit that ball over the roof, something no one else had been mighty enough to do, and it turned to a bird and flew away and dollar bills rained on the shanty poor. And I never even thought to get his autograph."

Hattie brings to the table plates of bacon and eggs, fried potatoes, bread toasted with butter in the oven, a pot of tea; and the three of us eat. It's late and I'm worried about Francene, but the food tastes good to me.

Is anything true? I wonder, envisioning the Babe's last homer metamorphosing into a bird, and money raining from the sky. A good story is better than truth. More real. Sometimes all that's left behind, all we have to go on.

"You know," Cooney says, "the Babe didn't really have a father to speak of and his mother died when he was still a boy. They sent him off to reform school."

"Why are you telling him this?" Hattie asks.

"Because there are worse things, poor little chap."

"Worse things than what, dear?"

"He received the Last Rites before he died."

Cooney is stone sober and that's what has me worried. He knows something about Francene. Something's wrong. She's not coming back. By now, she and George have crossed the Mississippi.

"You are the one who is getting maudlin, Cooney. You're going on as if you'd been at the jug."

"Let's have ourselves a little taste," Cooney says. "And then you and I, my dear, will take a turn about the dance floor."

Down in the cranberry-glass votive cups, candle wicks gutter in their wax soup, throwing shadows off the darkening walls occasionally lit by lightning flashes. Cooney, in the odd flicker, turns into Lon Chaney of *The Mummy*. The rain thrums steadily on the roof.

"I'd love to dance, but no whiskey. Please, dear?"

"'Please, dear,'" Cooney mimics. "I say we drink to the Babe."

"Not tonight, Cooney," says Hattie. "When will the lights come on?" There's a touch of panic in her voice.

Yet without the truth, people go crazy. Sustaining the narrative of what never happened, through constant revision and retelling, is too much to bear. Eventually the vessel cracks, and everything spills out.

"Will you have a drink with me, Bob?"

I don't know what to say.

"Don't be silly, Cooney. He's just kidding, Bobby."

"Kidding, I'm not."

"He's too young."

"Not by my lights he's not."

Cooney gets to his feet, rumbles over to a cabinet, and lowers a bottle of rye. Suddenly the lights come on—we shield our eyes—and Francene, utterly drenched, bursts in.

Her hair hangs like seaweed. Her face streams with water. She says how sorry she is for being so late, but she stopped at Gammon's for corned beef sandwiches. Then the power went out, so the trolleys couldn't run and she had to walk all the way home in the storm with no umbrella.

Cooney, holding the bottle of rye, gapes at her, and blurts, "Would you like a cup of tea, young woman?"

"Yes, you poor thing," says Hattie, "you're soaked to the bone."

"No. Thank you very much, but I think I'd better change clothes and then Bobby and I will have some supper. I'll bet he's starved."

I've never been happier in my life to see Francene, and I only realize when I see her how scared I was. Of everything. But I say, "I've already eaten."

"I brought corned beef sandwiches." She smiles a wet, thin smile.

"I'm full."

"Okay. Well, let's go. Thank you so much, both of you, for watching out for Bobby. I hope I haven't put you out."

"It's always a pleasure, Fran. We had the best time together. Didn't we, Cooney?"

"We did. We surely did," says Cooney as if convincing himself.

Back in our apartment she asks me another time if I wouldn't like a sandwich. They're still warm. She kept them dry under her jacket. When I tell her, "No," again, she drops them in the garbage can.

• • •

On October 6, Francene and I sit in front of our television set and watch the Lincoln Avenue episode of *Route 66*. The black mortuary across the street, the silver Corvette parked in our block, George and Martin Milner, the venerable Ethel Waters. There are trees, bushes, cobblestones, curbs and telephone wires we know intimately. Our neighborhood on screen is rarified, larger than it could ever be by just existing beyond our window, and when I look out at it, it pales to the flat, black-and-white TV version.

The show is sad. George and Milner speed across the map, searching for Ethel Waters' cronies as she dies, and we die with her. Each crag of her face and silver hair on her head, each murmur of her mouth pushes us closer to the end when Francene will emerge from that limo, hiding her broken heart behind a black dress, and stride bravely into the camera. Francene. Finally memorialized, like Angelina Colaizzi. Something that can never be taken away from her. The beginning of something big.

But she's not there. The limo never pulls up. Francene never gets out of it. Or if she is there, she's invisible. Lost. The last shot is of Our Lady's steeple. And then the band of strays plays triumphantly. All that brass, that low, tremulous, sad music until it's over and we are sitting there in front of a Marlboro commercial and there's simply nothing to say.

• • •

"Where's Carl?"

I look up from my milk. Standing there in the kitchen doorway with her hands on her hips is Virginia Mayo. Blonde. Restless and beautiful. Carnal in an obvious, almost brutal, way. As she stares at my beat-up face, everything about her softens and I see that it's Francene, with dyed blonde hair, rushing toward me.

"What in the world happened to you, Bobby?"

"I told Carl to get the hell out of here."

"Never mind, Carl. What happened to you? Who did this to you?" She's on her knees in front of my chair, her hand along my face.

"You were going to leave with him. Weren't you?"

"What are you talking about? He's just a friend. What happened to you? Were you in a fight? Who did this to you?"

"I don't feel good," I say.

"Oh, honey."

"I don't feel good."

How do you get what you want without asking for it with words that must come out of your mouth? Words you can't say even if you had been taught to say them. I feel like the guy who came back from the war with hooks instead of hands in *The Best Years of Our Lives*. Hattie said it perfectly: We all have funny ways of showing it.

I look into Francene's green eyes, her new blonde hair flowing about her movie star face, the red lips, the slightly open mouth with those outslanting teeth that make her look so fragile sometimes, and I see Poe shattering my stolen bat; the whole band of them lining up over Francene Renzo in the infield and dropping their pants; and I remember Mickey saying that he wanted to kill the nuns after they beat him.

"I hate your hair like this," I nearly shout.

"I'll change it back."

"I don't care what you do. You don't even go to Communion. What's wrong with you?"

Francene takes her hand from my face, and gets to her feet.

"What's wrong with me? I don't know what's wrong with me. I don't know why I don't go to Communion. What do you want me to say to you? I have nothing to say that will make a difference except that I'm doing my best even when it doesn't seem like it. This is as good as I am. What's lousy to other people is the top of my game. But if it makes you feel better, Bobby, then go ahead and attack. You think I'm not used to it? That I can't take it? Well, I can. I've been through it so many times that all it is for me is sitting through a bad movie. But, there are some things, boy, that you can learn to mind your own damn business about. I am your mother. I had you; you didn't have me. Now what happened to you today?"

I stare at this new Francene Renzo. Hard. Blonde. Her long monologue so much like a movie star's I'm not sure I know her or what will happen next.

"Nothing," I say.

"I'm not asking you. I'm telling you. What happened?"

Can I tell her that the beautiful black bat that I stole from Sears, a floor below where she stood working at the candy counter, was smashed into a thousand pieces? That Poe scratched a picture of her in the infield and a pack of boys pulled down their pants and got on top of it? What is it that I can tell her? That the eyes are on me? That I'm cursed? I don't care if she beats me, if she sends me to juvenile court. There's nothing I can tell her.

"Nothing," I say again. Then I cry. I cry. Like a child cries, full out, jubilant and unabashed, surprised that there is in me so much crying, surprised that I allow myself to be pulled into the arms of Francene Renzo, who sinks to the floor holding me.

Chapter 13

Aunt Lena cries when I ask Uncle Abe to be my Confirmation sponsor, then every few minutes she showers me with kisses. Uncle Abe says it's about time we made it official. Now we'll be *compadres*, and he'll have someone to leave all his money to.

Francene takes me to Sears, and with her employee discount, we buy a navy blue suit and necktie, white shirt and a pair of penny loafers. She buys a blue sailor dress and a big blue hat with a trailing sash.

On Saturday, May 11, the very day itself, Aunt Lena and Uncle Abe pick us up in their old, gray, two-door Plymouth. We park right in front of the church, get Uncle Abe situated with his wheelchair and oxygen, then I take off for my class.

Sister has told us over and over that Confirmation is the sacrament of Christian maturity. Surveying my classmates as Father Vita concelebrates the Mass with the Bishop, I fix on the girls who in their Confirmation frocks have metamorphosed miraculously into women before my eyes. The tide of their long, shining hair and chaste, untouched bodies fills me with wonder and foreboding, as if they are the communion of saints; and each time I bow my head at the spoken name of Jesus, as is required, I think just that precisely. *Jesus. Jesus. Jesus.* For one day, I know, as it is prophesied in the lives of boys, I will have one of them, and from now on I will never stop thinking about that day.

When it is time for the candidates to approach the altar, I fetch Uncle Abe and wheel him up the center aisle. He hums a barely audible version of "Take Me Out to the Ball Game." I look down at his sparse, wispy hair, like crayon hair in a child's drawing. That color brown. Waxy. At one point, he reaches back and pats my hand. His hand is bony and spotted, the wrist like a stick snaking out of the white cuff.

I kneel at the altar rail with my class as the Bishop approaches us. He is old and shaky, but he has about him a fury that his years of holiness and deprivation have varnished him with. He wears a tall green miter that quakes as he looks us over before beginning his interrogation.

Kneeling next to me is Patricia O'Connor, a long-blonde-haired, sky-blue-eyed girl in a pink dress and two gold bracelets. She is so pure that when she smiles a halo pops out of her head and hovers. I feel her next to me, like a column of levitating, white fire purging me of my catechism. I smell her. Lavendar and frankincense. I cannot tell if my lightheadedness is because of my proximity to Patricia or my terror that the answers to the questions the Bishop will surely direct at me have been burned away.

But the Bishop asks no questions. He merely dodders along the rail conferring the sacrament. When he gets to me, he addresses me by the new name I've chosen—*Luigi,* after Saint Louis—and says, "Receive the seal of the Holy Spirit, the Gift of the Father," as Uncle Abe places his hand upon my shoulder. With chrism, the old heavily-breathing Bishop slashes upon my forehead a cross and slaps my cheek, a reminder that I must be ready to endure hardship for my faith, and that for the rest of my life I am to imitate the virtues of the saint whose name I have adopted. Louis IX who became King of France at age twelve, led two crusades to the Holy Land, and regularly had supper with Saint Thomas Aquinas.

● ● ●

Francene and I have the home movie made at the party after my Confirmation. It sits in a flat tin film cannister at the top of a closet next to a hatbox of old, black-and-white family photographs where people, now dead, rehearse the truth of what never happened. We've never seen it. I don't even know who shot it. Nobody we know has a camera. But I remember those blinding lights, like searchlights, drilling into my eyes so that I couldn't see who was behind them.

Tonight we decide to watch it, so we check out a projector from the Carnegie Library, hang a bedsheet on the wall, and line up on the coffee table bowls of bridge mix, pistachios, and a long box of thin mints we keep chilled in the refrigerator.

The projector spasms and clicks. A ray of white light pours from it, and out of the light Uncle Abe and I appear. We shake hands. Exaggeratedly fast like a Charlie Chaplin movie. Uncle Abe is in his wheelchair, wizened and Oriental-looking, oxygen straws in his nose, smiling like a magician, dark suit and white tie, the very clothes he will be laid out in one month later.

A man whose head is cut from the frame passes behind us. He carries a brown pony bottle of Duquesne beer. Aunt Lena, holding a wriggling black-and-white spotted puppy, enters, the camera lights mirroring off her glasses. She hands the puppy to Uncle Abe, who then hands it to me. My Confirmation present from them. There's a quick shot of Francene, wide-eyed and smiling, shaking her fist in the direction of Uncle Abe, then back to me, trying to hold the wild little puppy, who chews on my tie.

I name him Pius, after the old pope. We have him only two weeks before Mr. Gigante, who is there at the party himself, wearing more jewelry than any of the women, smelling up the whole place with his cigars and eating every last one of Nonna's Tara Lucias, makes us get rid of him.

Baby doesn't like having another dog on the premises.
Francene declares we'll move, that sawed-off little *gavone*,
Gigante. But in the end there's no place really for us to go,
and we end up taking Pius to the Animal Rescue League
and leaving him.

The camera lands on the kitchen wall clock, stalled at
ten after four; the calendar next to it says May, 1963.
Francene is busy at the sink, her hair its native, ropey brown,
spread across the stars of her sailor dress's bib. She turns for
a moment and sticks out her tongue. There's a close-up of
the table. Platters of eggplant and pasta, salami and cheese
and bread, sausage and peppers, trays of Nonna's Italian
cookies, fruit, pitchers of wine and bottles of beer and pop.
Then a widening angle to take in everyone gathered around
it: Nonna, in black, smiling, holding a hand like a visor
above her eyes, the lights glinting off her gold crowns as
she smiles. Mr. and Mrs. D'Andrea in veils of cigarette
smoke, glasses of brackish forgetfulness before them. Hattie,
lifting her teacup from its saucer and dabbing at the corners
of her mouth with a napkin. Aunt Lena and Uncle Abe.

In my blue suit, tie loosened, I sit at the head of the
table like a boy patriarch, Pius across my knees, in one fist
a stack of folded money I've been given, and a bottle of
Lord Calvert in the other. I lift it to my mouth and
pantomime a long, impossible drink.

Around me my guests lift their glasses. They laugh and

smile. Their lips move. *Saluto,* they are toasting. *Benedire.*
Cento anni. A hundred years.

At the film's periphery, as through a scrim, others are
visible. Uninvited, black-and-white shadowgraph people
like film negatives. If I squint my eyes I can see them,
mingling with the others, smiling, filling plates, pouring
glasses of wine. But, surely, the living cannot see the dead.

Nonno is there, next to Nonna, smoking a diNobili,
his fish mustaches burnished with celluloid. Between them
sits Uncle John, jet black hair. The light knifes off his first
lieutenant's bars. His teeth are white as roots. He is too
handsome. Nonno can't stop kissing and petting him.

Cooney lumbers out of the murk, takes his place with
Hattie, and pours a shot of whiskey.

"Let us lift a glass to young Bob, lately come to
manhood." This is what he must be saying because everyone
rises and raises a glass. Even Uncle Abe struggles up from
his wheelchair and squeezes into the frame with me, still at
the tablehead with my own glass hoisted.

But I am not looking at them, but what is just at the
edge of the film beam, half-in and half-out, what they can't
seem to see. Mickey. Trying to smile, trying to stand on his
gnarled feet, and walk to me, the puppy leaping at his frail
cuffs and barking soundlessly.

A tall, spindly, white-shirted young man with horn-
rimmed glasses and thinning hair, so ascetic that you can

look straight through his gauzy chest at the picture of The Last Supper on the wall behind him, picks up the puppy. It writhes in his arms, licking his face until he smiles and sets it down. When Mrs. Zitelli hobbles with two canes into focus, I realize it is Hugo. He says something to Mickey, and together they walk out of the frame.

The camera races suddenly to Francene entering the room with a cake. She is unselfconsciously dazzling, flushed and beaming. Rita Hayworth, Elizabeth Taylor, Ava Gardner. All of them put together, and then some. Behind her, just a shade, a spackling of lights in the vague shape of a man, floats my father, burning away like smoldering newsprint. He never really comes into focus, but a hand for a moment materializes and reaches toward me, then disintegrates.

The scene shifts back to everyone, even the papery dead and the missing, still standing with drinks in the air, then on cue—*Saluto*—they bolt them down, their mouths working at what seems song, and clap for me still standing there trapped in the silent movie with the ceremonial shot in my hand.